It is notoriously diffic

THOMAS BURKE (1886-1945), and much of this is Burke's fault, as he often included inaccurate or contradictory accounts in his autobiographical writings. What does seem clear is that he was born in London—in suburban South London, not in the East End as has been sometimes suggested—and that his father died shortly after his birth. Burke's mother died when he was 10 or 11, and he was removed to the London Orphan Asylum, which he left around age 16 to work in an office. During his youth Burke seems to have become intimately familiar with the East End and the Limehouse district, a lower-class area inhabited largely by Chinese immigrants. His experiences and observations would lead to his first and biggest success, *Limehouse Nights* (1916), a collection of stories set in and around London's Chinatown. This volume was a substantial popular and critical success and went through numerous reprintings on both sides of the Atlantic; one of its tales was the basis for a 1919 D.W. Griffith film, *Broken Blossoms*. Burke continued to write prolifically, often returning to Limehouse, such as with *In Chinatown: More Stories from Limehouse Nights* (1921), *Whispering Windows: More Limehouse Nights* (1928), and *Abduction: A Story of Limehouse* (1939). *Night-Pieces* (1935) was something of a departure for Burke, featuring a collection of mostly crime and horror stories. The book was well reviewed, and Burke followed it up with the less successful *Dark Nights* (1944). In the decades following his death in 1945, Burke was remembered chiefly (if at all) for *Limehouse Nights*, but more recent critics, including S. T. Joshi and Jessica Amanda Salmonson, have recognized Burke's contributions to weird fiction, and a few of the stories in *Night-Pieces* are regularly included in mystery and horror anthologies.

COVER: The cover reproduces (Harold) Hookway Cowles (1896-1987)'s art for the front panel of the dust jacket of the British first edition, published by Constable in 1935. The same art was used for the 1936 American edition published by Appleton.

MORE VINTAGE THRILLS AND CHILLS FROM VALANCOURT

The Feast of Bacchus (1907) by Ernest G. Henham
The Mummy (1912) by Riccardo Stephens*
Benighted (1927) by J. B. Priestley
The Slype (1927) by Russell Thorndike
I Am Jonathan Scrivener (1930) by Claude Houghton
Man in a Black Hat (1930) by Temple Thurston
The Curse of the Wise Woman (1933) by Lord Dunsany
He Arrived at Dusk (1933) by R. C. Ashby
Hell! said the Duchess (1933) by Michael Arlen
The Cadaver of Gideon Wyck (1934) by Alexander Laing*
Harriet (1934) by Elizabeth Jenkins
Wax (1935) by Ethel Lina White
I Am Your Brother (1935) by Gabriel Marlowe*
The Deadly Dowager (1935) by Edwin Greenwood*
The Birds (1936) by Frank Baker
Fingers of Fear (1937) by J. U. Nicolson
Night and the City (1938) by Gerald Kersh*
The Hand of Kornelius Voyt (1939) by Oliver Onions
The Survivor (1940) by Dennis Parry
The White Wolf (1941) by Franklin Gregory
The Killer and the Slain (1942) by Hugh Walpole
The Master of the Macabre (1947) by Russell Thorndike
Brother Death (1948) by John Lodwick
The Feasting Dead (1954) by John Metcalfe
The Witch and the Priest (1956) by Hilda Lewis

* Forthcoming.

NIGHT-PIECES

Eighteen Tales by

THOMAS BURKE

VALANCOURT BOOKS

Night-Pieces by Thomas Burke
First published by Constable in 1935
First U.S. edition published by Appleton in 1936
First Valancourt Books edition 2016

Published by Valancourt Books, Richmond, Virginia
http://www.valancourtbooks.com

ISBN 978-1-943910-21-2 (trade paperback)
Also available as an electronic book.

All Valancourt Books publications are printed on acid free paper that
meets all ANSI standards for archival quality paper.

Set in Dante MT

CONTENTS

MIRACLE IN SUBURBIA

In a back room of one of the many old houses still left along London's southern riverside, an elderly man and a youth sat at a table and looked at each other. The man had a bird profile and a probing eye, and the hands that were clasped on the table were large and thin and white. The youth had no profile, and his hands were neither thin nor white, but large and red. They appeared to worry him. Once or twice he put them on the table, in imitation of the man's easy pose. Then he seemed to see them in comparison with the man's, and hid them. From time to time, as though they were forgetful of their unseemliness, they came again to the table, clasping and unclasping.

The room, too, seemed to worry him. It was an odd room; out of character with that stretch of the riverside; such a room as the youth had never seen there or elsewhere. He had seen museums and their contents. This room contained none of the things he had seen in museums, but it was filled with things that were not everyday furniture—queer things; and it had the feeling of a museum. He could not give names to the things; he knew only that he had never seen them in the British Museum or in South Kensington. Weird-looking things. Queer-shaped jars. Wooden sticks. Circular things. Triangular things. Yellow papers with all sorts of squiggles on them. He didn't like the look of them, but his eyes continued to rove about the room and return to them.

The man noted his uneasiness. "Have a drink?" He went to a sideboard, and began to get out some bottles.

The youth said hastily: "No-thanks. No-thanks. I—I'm not thirsty." He was not averse from a drink. He liked a drink with his friends. But he did not want a drink in this room with this man. Under his reason, under even his sense, he was aware that he was being warned not to have a drink here, not to stay here. The table warned him. The things hanging on the wall warned him. The window-curtains warned him. The very nostrils of the man talking to him warned him. The room seemed to be murmuring with distant drums. All the objects in it were throwing off something that went to the secret corners of his being, and said, "Have nothing to do with this place. Get out while you can."

But he couldn't be so silly as to make a sudden bolt; neither the man nor the room had so far afforded any reason for that. He would obey the feeling so far as to refuse a drink—you never knew with drinks; so easy to put something in 'em—but that urge to get out was probably just nerves. The man seemed quite a nice chap, and he couldn't *see* anything wrong with the room. There was no danger anywhere; nobody was threatening him. If the man tried to attack him, that would be different. That'd be a reason for getting out. But a mere "feeling" was silly, and the feeling that he had about this room was probably due to his not having seen a room like it before. He must fight it down. The man had said he had a proposal to make which might be profitable to the youth, and the youth could do with a proposal or two of that sort. He mustn't allow "feelings" to interfere with business.

"Well, if you won't have a drink," the man was saying, "let's get on with our talk. I spoke to you in the coffee-shop just now because you looked a likely lad for the work I want done. A simple piece of work, and I'd pay well. H'm."

"I could do with a job. Been out nearly a year now. Tramping about every day looking for something. Can't find anything, though."

"No? I thought that was the case. Well, now, I just want a little bit of work done, and I'll pay for it what you'd probably have to work half a year for in the ordinary way. For this piece of work, which you can do in an hour or two, I'll pay you—fifty pounds."

"Fifty pounds?"

"Fifty pounds."

The youth seemed to try to visualize fifty pounds—fifty pounds all at once. The picture, and the effort to produce it, made him frown. He became suspicious. "Fifty pounds. . . . Must be something queer if you'd pay all that. Fifty pounds. . . . Must be something not right."

The man smiled. "I like your recoil. I appreciate it. But you need have no hesitation on that score. The answer to your remark is, in a sense, yes and no. That is, a little technical point of what is called wrong-doing is involved. But not the kind of technical point that could get you into trouble. Just a matter of—" he laughed—"taking something from somebody. But listen!" He held up a hand to stop the youth's protest. "Taking something from somebody who stole it. A perfectly honourable proceeding. An act that a dozen men of spotless respectability would be willing to perform, if they were young enough and agile enough. And I'm willing to pay fifty pounds—sums of money convey little to me, though I realize that they mean something to others—because I need a young man whom I can trust. A young man to whom fifty pounds would be a symbol of a vow of silence. That was why I picked on you. It's like this."

He leaned back in his chair and held the youth with his eyes. The youth frowned again in the effort of concentrating on what might be a complicated story. "A very valuable relic has been taken from a museum with which I'm connected. If we make the loss public we're likely to lose it. It will go abroad. We want no publicity; no scandal. We want simply to get it back. We know who has it and where it is. And a smart young man could get it without any trouble. And would do a service to society. And—further—without any danger to himself whatever."

"Oh ..." The youth pondered. It sounded all right, but coming from this particular man it didn't seem quite as right as it sounded. He was an honest youth, and never would have eased his troubles even by the lightest of crimes. Yet this man's eyes and voice swayed him. It seemed that he was asked to perform a straightforward, but not quite proper, service, and was to be handsomely paid for it and protected from all risk. Well, if it *was* all right, fifty pounds was fifty pounds. Without that handsome reward he would have said no to the proposal, even if the act was a service to society. He was not a hero, and saw no reason for implicating himself in other people's troubles. On the other hand, if it was not all right, a reward of a thousand pounds and complete immunity would not have tempted him to common theft. He couldn't quite "get" this man. His chief feeling was that it wasn't all right, but under this man's eyes he couldn't feel that it was wrong. It seemed to be a private row about public property, and if that was so his moral sense told him that he would be justified in accepting the job and restoring the thing, whatever it was, to its owners. Still, there were one or two funny points about it.

"But if it's all right and above board, and as easy as you say, why are you paying all that money for the job?"

"I've told you. Fifty pounds probably seems a lot of money to you, but it's nothing to the historic value of this relic. Anyway, I should not be paying that money for the mere job. I should be paying it, as I said, for a man's honesty and for his keeping quiet. This matter must not be talked about to anybody. It's a delicate matter. Might lead to trouble with other countries. You understand? That's why I need somebody who knows nothing of the circumstances surrounding the affair, and somebody who will forget it after he has performed his service. Somebody who will never mention that service—nor what the object of the service was. Particularly that. No mention of the nature of the relic."

"I'm not much of a talker at any time."

"I've observed that on my visits to the coffee-shop."

"But what's this about no trouble and no danger? How can that be? If I'm taking something from another chap, he naturally wouldn't let me. Or what about a copper seeing me do it?"

"Even if you were seen taking it, nobody could harm you. You will be protected. You will approach that man freely and you will come away freely. I have power to protect you, and my power will accompany you all the time."

"Power? You mean some of your people—some of those interested in the thing?"

The man smiled. "I see you don't understand. And perhaps it's as well you don't. You will be more efficient for the work. But there are powers other than the powers of the hands and limbs. There are powers other than the powers of the brain. There is a power of the spirit. That is the power that will protect you."

"Mmm. . . . Sounds all right. So do lots o' things. But if you got all this—what you call power, I should think you could get it back easy enough yourself. Just say, 'Presto, come over here,' like the conjurers." He giggled. Was this old chap drunk—him and his talk about taking things from people and being protected by power?

"I see you don't understand. And don't believe. We who have this power may not use it ourselves. We may use it only through an instrument. *Then* it is effective. And no harm can come to our instrument. We can place our protective power around him."

"How d'you make that out? S'posing the chap that's got this thing goes for me, and——"

"If he does, no harm can come to you. You do not believe, and it is not really necessary that you should. But perhaps I may convince you. Look, I am putting my power around you now. I am calling up the power within you. Now!"

He pushed back his chair and stood erect, looking down at the youth. For some seconds they stared at each other. In the moment of his rising the man's body seemed to fill the room and to be bursting from it. The lamp on the mantelshelf threw its shadows enormously on the wall, and the shadows copied their movements and became a secondary couple engaged in silent, sinister business. The youth was faintly sensible of some disturbance of the air; then of some change in himself—a feeling of confidence and strength.

The first instinct was that the man was putting something over on him. He resented this, and wasn't going to have it. He was glad he hadn't had that drink. But with the feeling of confidence his resentment passed. This was good. This wasn't the hypnotism he had heard about. He wasn't this man's dumb servant; he was his equal. He felt that all the things he had often seen himself doing, he could do; that he had abilities which he hadn't even guessed at but which this man perceived. He felt as though up to now he had been tied up; an inarticulate, ineffectual youth; and that this man had released him. He stretched both hands on the table, no longer ashamed of them, leaned back, and stared at the man.

"You feel something? ... Ah.... That is my power meeting your power—blending with it and clothing you. You doubted what I said. It is natural that you should. These things are known to few. But now you are doubting your own doubts. My power is over you. And you are aware of it. Now I will convince you utterly that if you serve me in this matter you will be protected from every kind of harm. See!"

In one rhythmic movement the man swung to the wall, tore down from it a naked Turkish sword, whirled it above his head with a long arm, and brought its edge, full swing, down upon the youth's right wrist.

The youth said "Oo, I say!"

"Hurt you?"

"No. Give me a start, like. Wasn't expecting you to do that."

"Ha! Look at that blade's edge. Feel it."

"Jee! Blooming razor." Then he seemed to realize that something odd had happened. His voice rose to a squeak. "Here—but —but you slashed that across my wrist with all your might. You —you—A thing like that'd cut through a table. And you——"

"I did. Look at your wrist."

The youth examined the wrist. "Can't see anything. Not a mark even."

"Of course not. Didn't I tell you that my power was protecting you? Give me one of those logs from that box by the fire."

The youth took up an oak log-wedge of twelve-inch thickness —and placed it on the table. "Now see. My power is not protecting that log, and so——" He made a second swing of the sword and brought it down on the log. The log fell in two pieces.

The youth stared. "Jee!"

"That sword, as you say, would cut through a table. But it cannot cut through you. Nothing could. Nothing can in any way harm you. Between danger and you stands my power. And so you can do this little business for me—er—and my colleagues with no more risk than you would face in walking from here to your home. Does this evidence convince you?"

The youth's face was blank. His sense and brain were in effervescence. "Well, if blooming miracles is evidence . . ."

"It was not a miracle—in your sense. It was a fact. What is commonly called a miracle is only a fact of applied knowledge. Now, will you do a little bit of work for us?"

"Well, if it's absolutely straight—yes. But I don't want to be mixed up in any funny stuff."

"It *is* absolutely straight. The circumstances of the affair prevent my giving you proof of that. You must take my word for it. That you will be guaranteed against all danger I have already proved. Nobody need be ashamed of performing such a service as this—the recovery of a valuable relic for its owners. . . ."

"Well, what do you want me to do? And what is this thing?"

"The thing—" the man lowered his voice, and for a moment seemed to lose the suggestion of bulk—"the thing is a porcelain goblet."

"Porce—*what?*"

"A por—a china jar. A simple china jar. But very old. And of great historic value. You will simply take it from the man and bring it here."

"Simply take it. . . . And what'll he do?"

"He may make some resistance, but no matter what he does he cannot harm you. I thought I had made that clear."

"Yes . . . yes . . . er . . . I see. You mean there might be a schemozzle but me being like I am now, his stuff won't come off. Like the sword? That's it, eh?"

"That's it exactly."

"Don't hardly seem able to believe it. More like a dream."

"Well, you have had proof with the sword. And you will have further proof. Now follow your instructions. . . . At half-past eleven to-night a man will come from a house in Sloane Street and walk along Sloane Square. A short man in spectacles, wearing a fawn overcoat and bowler hat. He will be carrying an attaché case. If he is not carrying a case the—er—jar will be in his overcoat pocket. He will go through that narrow street by the District station—he will be making for Pimlico Road. When he is in that narrow street, you will approach him and snatch the case, or take the jar from his pocket, and bring it here to me."

The youth, stirred by this picture of daring doings, giggled. "Sounds easy."

The man folded his arms and looked at him with cold eyes. "It *will* be easy."

The youth got up. "Y'know, I believe it will. You could make a chap believe anything in this room. I don't understand it, but after that sword. . . ."

"Good. I see that you believe, and that you know you can do what I want. Here—" He put a hand inside his coat and brought out a bundle of treasury notes. "Fifty, if you count them, I think."

The youth stared. "Caw! This is a rum joint. Paying me before I've earned it. Before I've done the job."

"You will earn it. I am passing this over as proof of *my* good faith. Your good faith will be proved by your performance."

"But s'pose I was to bunk with the bag?"

"You will not bunk with the bag. For one thing, you are not that kind of young man. I know you. Anyway, the bag would not be worth five shillings, and the—the china jar has no commercial value. You could not sell it. But I——" For a moment he forgot the youth, and again he seemed to fill the room. "I, with that goblet, am lord of all beauty. With the Bool Museum goblet, I am lord of all——"

"You're how much?"

He recovered himself. "Er—I said claiming that goblet is a laudable duty."

"But s'pose I was copped by a motor-bus and smashed up?"

He made a *tch* of irritation. "How many times am I to tell you that so far as this matter is concerned, you are under protection. Now and always. You cannot be harmed by anything arising from this matter—neither now nor at any time. I am protecting you. Now are you ready?"

The youth made but a momentary hesitation. Then—"Yes, I'll do it."

"Good. It is now half-past ten. You have plenty of time for the journey to Sloane Square. You have your instructions. Make no mistake in them. I shall expect you back soon after twelve." He opened the door and led the way into the passage, and so to the front door.

The youth walked out with light step and swinging shoulders. His gaze was direct and his movements sharp. Within the last hour he had developed a profile. He was not aware of this himself; he was aware only that he was "feeling fine." Whether this was due to the fifty pounds in his pocket, to the thing he had witnessed in that room, or to something else, he did not know. He was content to feel fine and to go upon his errand.

As he went, he chuckled in self-communion. "Jee! Talk about the age of miracles. If anybody'd told me I'd a-seen a thing like that in these streets. . . . He's a Dr. Caligari, he is. Almost fright-

ens you, seeing a thing like that. And yet it don't. I don't feel that
way at all. Going to do a hold-up and get away with it. Still, he
says it's all right. Only taking something from a thief for them
it belongs to. Wonder if it does belong to 'em? Still, he seems all
right. And I made it clear I wouldn't touch it if it wasn't straight. I
got a clear conscience on that. And I got me fifty pounds anyway.
Better drop that at home on me way. Case there's anything sticky
about the business, and it goes wrong. Then at least they'll have
that to help 'em. But I reckon it'll be all right. He *makes* you feel
everything's all right."

At half-past eleven he was waiting in the shadow by the Sloane
Square District station. He had been there for fifteen minutes,
waiting for the half-hour with no more trepidation than if he
were waiting for a bus. He was wondering no more about the
business; he seemed to be outside it, half-asleep. His mind would
not be interested in it; even when the man appeared his pulse remained unchanged.

The man appeared at three minutes past the half-hour. He
came into the Square from Sloane Street—a small man in spectacles, wearing a fawn overcoat and bowler hat, and carrying an
attaché case. He walked softly, his eyes primly fixed on the pavement. He passed the youth without raising his eyes, and turned
into the side-street. The youth followed, as casually as though he
were merely walking that way, too.

Then, in the middle of the street, where the light was dim, he
moved more quickly. A few paces brought him right behind the
man. One hand, with a clean flash, grabbed the man's wrist; the
other snatched the case.

That was easy. What would happen next he did not know, but
he turned to make swiftly, without running, for Sloane Square.
But this was not to be so easy. Before he had taken three paces the
man was upon him. Two iron arms, unexpected from so slight
a man, went round him. He staggered on his heels. One of the
arms slid down his arm to reach the case. He closed his fingers
over its handle, and gave a violent backward kick. It met a shin,
and with its impact, there was a moment's easing of the arms.
The youth took that moment to slip through the arms downward
to the ground.

With his free arm he caught the man behind the knees, and they came down together. Silent, save for their gasping, they rolled on each other across the pavement. The man did not strike him, but fought for the hand that held the case. The youth held to it fiercely, struggling to rise. Then, with a sudden movement from the man, he found himself underneath, lying on his back with his neck against the curb. He made a few sharp struggles to reverse the positions, but within a second or so he saw that they were useless, and his throat went dry.

The dim light had shown him the man's hand shooting to his coat. Next moment he saw the hand lifted, and alongside the hand the dim light was caught by the blade of an open razor.

The youth's left hand still clutched the case. With his right he made a feeble effort to hold the man away, but the man, with his strong left, bent the arm back. The youth saw the razor sweeping down. Instinctively he shut his eyes. He felt the razor slash across his neck. He felt it go deep into each side. He gurgled and was aware of floating away.

It was a mere muscular movement that caused him to open his eyes, and it was then that he remembered what he had momentarily forgotten—that he was under protection. He opened his eyes to see that the man, half-squatting, had drawn back from him and was staring at him—at his neck—with eyes in which was a light of horror. With another instinctive movement the youth put his hand to his neck. His neck was whole. No wound. No pain. The man still held the open razor and looked stupidly at it. It was spotless.

Gripping the case, the youth rolled over and got to his feet. The man scrambled up with him and held out a hand. "Here— my case—my case." It was a plea more than a demand. The youth ignored it. He moved away, and the man with the strong arms put out a weak hand to detain him. "My case—my case."

Round the corner came a constable. He looked at their dusty clothes and torn collars. "What's all this? What's this?"

The youth answered him. "It's all right. Just a private dust-up. We're moving on now."

"Do it then."

The man tried to say something. "He—he—he——" and seemed unable to find further words.

"Well, what did he do?"

"He—he—he——"

"Now come on. Pack up and get home. And take more water with it."

The youth said, "All right," and went easily toward Sloane Square with the case. Behind him he heard the little man saying "No, but he—he—he——" and the constable saying, "Come on now—take a walk." He saw the constable wave the little man toward Pimlico Road, and he saw the little man tamely go.

On the platform of the District station he waited for an eastbound train. Four times while waiting he said, "Jee!" Not in a mood of chuckling but in a mood of awe. He felt a little sick—not because he had been wounded but because he hadn't been wounded.

Half an hour later he delivered the case to the old man and went home. He got into bed! with a blunt prayer—Jee!

For the next week life was good to him. Out of his vast store of fifty pounds, he used half-crowns and five-shillings at a time, presenting them to his mother as wages he had received for odd jobs. He took in delicacies for her tea. He bought his young sister a needed pair of boots. He saw prosperity ahead. Before it was exhausted he would certainly get a job; one bit of luck always led to another. Or with that capital he might start a little business. Or with ten or fifteen pounds of it he might go into partnership with a stall-holder.

Anyway, he was on his feet again, and all through meeting that—he almost thought of him as That Old Bonehead—a name which he and his friend, Fred, had used when discussing the old man in the coffee-shop. But after what had happened he couldn't use that term. He was a little afraid; it would be like mocking thunder and lightning. Something more respectful was needed, but he couldn't think of any word that would fit such an overwhelming man. The only events he knew comparable with what had happened were those he had learned of in religious lessons in school—making the sun stand still and those chaps that walked in the furnace. And you couldn't quite put a man who lived three streets away from you in an everyday suburb, in that class. That was Holy, and this man wasn't Holy. On the other hand, he must certainly be the most wonderful man in the world. He compromised by thinking of him as The Wonderful Old Man.

Once or twice during the week he felt a little twinge in his neck. But when he examined it in the mirror there was nothing to be seen; just a clean white neck, as usual. He concluded that the little man must have gripped his neck before he struck, and given a slight sprain to a small bone. You got that kind of thing sometimes at football on Saturdays, and often didn't feel it till the middle of the next week. After the second twinge, he ignored it, and went cheerfully about his plans for laying out his money.

Nine days after his little adventure he had his seven-o'clock tea, with two kippers, and then went into the parlour of their little four-room home, to read the evening paper and a book he had borrowed from the Free Library—a book which he found hard to read but which he wanted to read: a book on the Magic of the Ancients.

Half an hour later his friend Fred called. The youth's mother opened the door to him. "Hullo, Fred."

"Hullo, Mrs. Brown. Joe in?"

"Yes. He's in the parlour, reading, I think."

"Got a bit of news for him. He ever tell you about an old man we've met in Harry's coffee-shop?"

"No. Not that I remember."

"Ah. You hear a bang just now?"

"Might have. Yes, I believe I did. But there's all sorts of bangs around here. Lorries back-firing and that. You don't notice 'em."

"Well, the old man's blown himself up."

"Blown himself up?"

"Yes. Making some experiment, I suppose, and blown the house and himself all to bits. The whole front of the house. Blown clean out. I just come from it. There's crowds staring at it. Thousands. I thought Joe might like to come and have a look."

"Ah. Well, you'll find him in there. I must get on with me washing."

Fred opened the parlour door and stepped in, beginning his story with "I say, Joe, there's a——" And then Mrs. Brown heard a scream. She bustled into the passage. "What's the matter, Fred? Whatever's the matter?"

Fred stepped back into the passage with white face and open jaws. He put out an arm. "Don't go in. Don't go. Keep out."

"Why—why? What—what is it?"

But Fred could only say—"Don't—don't go in. His throat! His throat!"

YESTERDAY STREET

Dominic left the taxi at the foot of the High Street, and settled himself to look up the length of the street from the station to the Park. Its features met his eye so familiarly that, though forty years had passed since he last walked along it, he felt that he had left it but a month ago. There had been little rebuilding. He saw motors and taxis in place of carriages and cabs, and motor-buses and electric trams in place of the old horse-vehicles, and a movie-theatre where the Gospel Hall had been.

But there, unchanged, was the draper's whose Christmas windows had been his delight. There, too, were the little side-streets, changed only in the direction of creeping shabbiness; and there was the very sweet-stuff shop which had once had his halfpennies and pennies, its window arranged precisely as in the past. There was the Diamond Jubilee Clock Tower. There was the Italian restaurant. And there was the confectioner's, whose window, occupied each December by a Christmas cake of twelve huge tiers, had been one of the Christmas sights of North London.

Noting these points, he thought, as all men think on Going Back—Had he really been away forty years? Or did he only fancy it? Had all those things—what he called his Life—really happened to him, or had he only invented them as something he would like to happen? Had he really lived in a dozen countries, and was he really rich and living in a suite at the Palermo? Funny thing, growth.

Often, in the past, he had thought of the place, and of the boy who used to live in it, but the thought had been merely abstract and perfunctory; he hadn't been interested. Now, with his feet on its stones, he found how easily he could recapture it all, and how thickly long-buried memories perked up. The confectioner's, bearing the same name and the same fascia front as in his day, reminded him that he used to buy there, from a table in the doorway, assortments of yesterday's cakes—two or three for a penny.

And with that came memory of a crime, when once, in buying a pennyworth, he had, by sleight of hand, gone off with five instead of three. He looked away from the shop; he had an idea that the back of his neck was blushing. Two shops into which he could see had, in his day, been kept by erect, slightly-grey men, with beards. It had been the custom, he remembered, to slip into the doorways of those shops and shout "Kruger!" and run. They were now kept, he noted, by bald, withered men; but in the movements of those men he recognized the terrifying seniors of his own day. He felt that if they looked at him he would run.

He turned and went slowly up the street, noting on right and left many a familiar name. He tried to discover the effect upon him of seeing again a crude kind of life with which for years he had had nothing to do, and at first he could not locate or name it, definite though it was. Then, as he went farther into the street, he found that he felt, of all things, just a little frightened. Yes; it *was* a little frightening to re-cross the threshold of the past, and to see again so much of the furniture of his early life in the position in which he had left it. There it stood, as though in a locked room, just as when he had said farewell to it (as he thought, for ever) and had left his boyhood there, and entered youth and manhood elsewhere. Walking among it now, unlocking it, as it were, he caught all the stored odours of that boyhood, and half-wished that the street had been pulled down and rebuilt. For of these buildings almost every one had known him and had received something of him. Through forty years he had been moving, changing, widening his interests, seeing and hearing new things, and living six different kinds of life. While here, static and scarcely touched by the forty years which had given him forty outlooks and a million emotions, here were the relics and fixtures of the beginning of it all—a beginning he had until now forgotten.

Strolling up to the Clock Tower, the thought came to him that with the High Street almost as it was, the little fountain still there, the Park just as it was, and those two old men still there, it was possible that his own street was still there—Levant Street, wasn't it? And just possible that his very home was still there—the little cottage with the tiny front garden. And even possible that the garden had the same flowers—London Pride, he thought they were. In coming here he had had no thought of seeking out his home; he had assumed that it would long ago have been swept away. He had come merely to look at the old suburb, though he couldn't have said why he wanted to look at it; why the fancy, or rather imperative desire, should suddenly have possessed him on this particular morning to go and look at it. For the past ten years he had made extended visits to London three times a year, and never once had he even thought of coming here. Yet this morning the fancy to see the place had been so strong that he had meekly followed it. Now that he was here, and so little change had happened, he decided to look for Levant Street. With all the other old stuff and old people still here, it was quite likely that the street and the old cottage were still here. Where forty years had left no mark, anything was possible. Everything about the place, he thought, was so set and solid, that it even wouldn't surprise him to find the boys still there—just as he had left them—Jimmy Gregory, his special friend, and—who was it?— yes, Victor Jones —and—ah, yes—Jenny Wrenn. The High Street and the shops hadn't grown up, so perhaps. . . .

He shook his shoulders. Stop it. You're getting morbid. You're a bit depressed at Coming Back, and finding it all as it was. One ought to be able to look at it coldly—as a cast-off skin. But one can't. Funny. . . . Street looks bright enough, and yet it's all—somehow—melancholy. Aching. As though there were a shadow behind it, pressing on me. Pulling me and claiming me.

He stopped by the brown granite pillars of the familiar grocery store, and here his mind began to waver between the man he was, with his affairs centred in a suite at the Palermo, and the boy he had been. For a while he could not fix himself in either. Then, staring about the street, he found that his visual memory had called up the faces of those boys and their clothes, and his ear had called up their voices, not vaguely, as in reverie, but vividly. And Jenny Wrenn. Little Jenny Wrenn, the fourth party of the quartet. It was the thought of her, on this spot, and the clear image of her, that for a space blurred the fact of his Palermo life, and took him right back. The forty years, the travel, the experience, and the money, now slid out of his mind and left it empty, save for three boys and a girl in these streets.

Memories fell upon him as sharply and as separately as rain-drops. How many times he had come with her, or she with him, to this very store, each pretending to assist the other in "errands" for their mothers? And how many times they had gone laggingly home in the winter twilight, hand in hand, and silent. Jenny Wrenn in her blue-and-white pinafore and darned stockings and red tam o' shanter. Jenny Wrenn with the brown hair and the solemn eyes and the trick of standing on one leg and nursing the ankle of the other in her hand. How often they had stood together at dark corners, thrilling to the music of a street-organ. How often she had brought him buttonholes of marigolds from her front garden. How often they had waited for each other after school and gone on forbidden walks in the Park. How often they had "joined" things—the Band of Hope, the Sunday School—so that they might be more together.

He was letting these memories come to him on the pavement outside the store, when, in one special moment, there came with the memories the odour and flavour of strawberries and cream —and so potently that the dish might have been in his hands. He recalled then that their last meeting had been over a feast of strawberries and cream provided for them by the childless and "comfortable" widow, Mrs. Johnson, in honour of his leaving school and going away.

Following this came a sharp memory of a long-distant summer. Had the memory come when he had left his taxi, it would have been of something from a remote world and of another creature; but outside this store it came to him as inti-mately as last week. It was a summer when he and Jenny Wrenn had been sent together for a fortnight at a farm in Surrey. He recalled fourteen days and evenings of bliss. Of climbing trees, and lying in the sapphire dusk of the wood, and knocking each other about, and getting bad-tempered, and calling each other nasty names, and "making it up." He recalled the afternoon when he had buried her too deeply in the hay, and she had struggled out and fought him with real hatred. And he recalled those quiet half-hours in the coppice before bed-time, when they had sat on a low branch of a tree and stared at the country, and held hands, and didn't know why.

Fourteen days and evenings of bliss; two hundred and twenty-four hours of active being, every ten minutes of which had been *lived*. Since those days he had given much of his leisure to poetry, and had even played at the practice of it. But though to-day his mind was stored with it, and though as a boy he had known nothing about it, he realized now that he had known something better. He had known poetry itself, and had lived it. He wondered again whether he had ever really had any life than that; and then he was irritated with himself for wondering such nonsense. He moved away from the store and jerked himself back to his every-day, and wished he hadn't come to this dilapidated suburb.

He decided that he wouldn't stay long. He had a lunch appointment at the Palermo with some friends who had never seen this London suburb, and could not have said where it was; friends who had never played marbles in a side-street. He would just go along and see if Levant Street was still there, and then he would find a taxi and get out of this place which, much against his expectation, was so depressing and disarranging him. He had thought to look at it with superior eyes—success kindly glancing at its early beginning; but it wasn't following the rules. It was gripping him and reclaiming him. If he had guessed that it would be doing this to him he wouldn't have obeyed that sudden wish and wasted a morning on it. However, now he was here, he would just take a look at the old street, if it was still there, and then get back to civilization.

He strolled along the High Street to the point where he remembered his street had stood, and with not much surprise he found it still there. Where, in his day, the corner shops had been a cheap greengrocer's and a cheap butcher's, they were now a tobacconist's and a cheap draper's; but generally the silhouette of the street was the same. At the top end was a new row of flats, but beyond them still stood the school and the little houses with their tiny front gardens.

He stood for a moment looking into it, and again the Palermo and the rest of his life was swept out of his mind, and again, as he entered the street, a troop of things-past entered and took possession of him, and changed him from the serious figure known to many serious people into just Don, a boy of thirteen. He entered it with timid, hesitating steps, and the "frightened" feeling was a little stronger here than it had been in the High Street. From the school downward, the rest of its length held all the points it had held forty years ago. The little front gardens, some trim, some neglected; the Chapel; the little shops; the tiny public-house; and the one house which belonged to a century ago, set back behind a carriage-sweep, empty in his day and empty now.

Before each of these points he paused, his mind dazzled by a confetti of memories which the sight of each showered upon him. Then, very slowly, he moved on to look for number 64, and point by point—each clearly remembered—he came to it. There it was—almost as he had left it. Number 64, the little house which had been his first home. And sure enough, its garden was still bright with London Pride. He crossed the street and stood before it. Smaller, of course, than when he was a boy. He had expected that. Windows which look large to children, and knockers which only an effort can lift, become minute when seen again through the eyes of manhood. But, though smaller, it was still itself. The wooden palings, the fanlight, and the cobblestone edging to the bed of London Pride were just as he had left them. In imagination he looked beyond its door and saw the little rooms which had known him so intimately; which had known his first breath and his first dreams, and which held, as it were, the spiritual fingerprints of the creature he had been and now was not, and yet was. In that little house were preserved, as in acid or in amber, all the little moments, the particles of himself, which he had given it.

And as he stood before it, it seemed to him that all those particles came rushing out to greet him, bringing with them excitement, amusement, sadness, and here and there a touch of shame. Here, even more clearly than in the High Street, he could see himself; and it was disconcerting thus to see himself. Between the two, that self and this self, he was aware of reproach, regret, disappointment, weariness.

He did not look long. He stayed only for an aching minute; then turned away. But in turning away he sent a glance down the street towards other of the little houses where he had been a guest of school-friends.

And then, with head half-turned, he stumbled off the kerb, and was only half-aware that he had stumbled. He did not step back to the kerb. He stood where he was and kept his glance where it was. His glance was held by the little house numbered 82, and he gave it even more attention than he had given to his own house. His mind spoke the number, "Eighty-two." Yes; that was right. That had been her house.

He stepped back to the pavement and continued to gaze at number 82. He could not take his eyes from number 82, because, outside number 82, leaning against the wooden gate of the little garden, filled, as in the past, with marigolds, was a slim figure in red tammy and blue-and-white pinafore, standing on one leg.

*   *   *   *

Manhood had taught him to control all outward expression of emotion, and the two people who were then passing saw only a middle-aged man stepping on to the pavement and looking idly at the houses opposite. They saw no staring eyes or pursed lips or rutted frown, but his mental state was that which some people express in this way. His face and eyes were calm; it was the spasm that went across his chest and down his spine which was the private equivalent of staring eyes and pursed lips. The resemblance of the scene to the scenes of forty years ago was so acute that for a few moments he could only pace up and down. The very house—and outside it a child matching in every detail, so far as he could see, the Jenny Wrenn who had lived there and had been his sweetheart. It was so striking a likeness that in default of any other explanation he wondered whether his Jenny Wrenn could still be there and this child her grand-daughter. If she were there, he wondered whether he could face her, and decided that he couldn't, and again wished he hadn't come.

But, being here, he wanted to know; so, under pretence of examining the numbers of the houses, he began to cross the street. He did not wish to embarrass or scare the child by looking closely at her, but he wanted a nearer view. He proposed to pass her, and pause, and ask if she knew a Mrs.—he would invent a name. But he had scarcely reached the middle of the road when he stopped. From that point he could see something which made the likeness frighteningly exact. There, on the brown stocking of the left leg, was the selfsame darn in black wool which he remembered, had so distressed his Jenny's sense of fitness. At sight of that, the "frightened" feeling which this coming-back had inspired reached its crisis and became panic. He felt that he must get out of that street—and quickly.

But he was not allowed to get out. Even as he turned she removed any scruple he had had of embarrassing or scaring her, and offered him every chance of looking closely at her. She came forward from the gate, and stepped into the road, and stood in front of him. Then as she stood there, swinging one leg backward and forward in the familiar way, a hotter spasm went across his chest. Jenny Wrenn looked at him and smiled and said: "Hullo, Don. Where you been? Jimmy Gregory's looking for you."

Standing in the middle of the road, he stared deep into the young face; stared for some seconds. Then, forgetting his panic, forgetting himself and all rule and all law, he said, without thinking and very softly: "O-oh . . . It's really *you*. You're still here?" The screwed-up black eyes gave him a mischievous smile. Through the smile she said: "Why, of course. Look—Jimmy Gregory wants you."

He turned; and there, in the school playground, was Jimmy Gregory, waving to him and running. And down the street he saw Victor Jones coming towards them with his usual weary slouch. And, as both boys approached them, Jenny sidled up to him and leaned upon him, as she always did; and in that moment he was no more depressed or frightened or amazed. The common air of that little street became in that moment a great and gentle wave of peace and well-being which poured upon him and through him. Lacing the air, was the faint odour of strawberries and cream.

*   *   *   *

One little spot of everyday remained with him to tell him that the oddest thing about all this was that none of them seemed to recognize that he was grown-up, or to pay any attention to his gold-headed cane and his slim, brilliant boots. They treated him as they always had treated him. He looked up the street to the point where it entered the High Street, and he saw that everything of the High Street was as it was five minutes ago—taxis, motor-buses, electric trams—and that the little houses among which they stood were showing wireless aerials. Yet there they were, the four of them, making a casual cluster in the roadway, as usual, giggling and talking of this and of that—of what their teacher had said or done that morning; of the magic-lantern show at the Chapel last night; of the coming Band of Hope Treat. They were all going that evening—all four of them—to get their tickets for the Treat, and he found himself telling them that he had heard that part of the Treat would be a nigger entertainment. From somewhere unseen came the pathetic music of a street-organ. It was playing a popular song of their time—a song he had once thought "lovely"—*Little Dolly Daydream.* Jenny began twinkling her feet to its time.

The last remnants of his to-day self slipped from him. He found it impossible to think, and, having tried, found that he didn't want to. He was caught in some silver-silken net, and he was content to be caught. He couldn't bother to make out what had gone wrong (or perhaps right) with Space and Time; he accepted as a fact that the modern world was all about him, and that here he was with his gold-headed cane and the children he had known long ago. And they were real; visible and touchable. He tested this by giving a gentle tug at one of Jenny's curls, as he had often done. She replied by jerking her head and butting his arm —hard enough to hurt. After that, he was conscious of nothing save that he was Don among his old friends, with a faint memory of having been other things.

Jimmy Gregory nudged him. "Got your marbles?" He said: "No. Left 'em indoors." "All right—lend you some of mine. You can pay what you lose after dinner."

Then he and Jimmy Gregory were crouched in the roadway playing marbles, and Jenny was stooping over them, with brown curls hanging, bubbling rude remarks about his bad play; and he was very happy. He found, while playing, that his gold cane *had* been noticed, and that, most oddly, they did not question it or appear to regard it as unusual. Jenny took it from him—"I'll hold that stick while you're playing—or trying to."

At the end of the game he had lost heavily. He had borrowed

ten of Jimmy Gregory's marbles, and, despite a few fluking wins, which at one time gave him sixteen, had lost the lot. "That's ten," Jimmy said; and Dominic said: "That's right. I'll bring 'em out after dinner. See you before class." "That's all right."

Jenny wanted to know what he was going to have for dinner, but he had no information. He never had known until he got home. Jenny reported that she had seen her mother preparing a large steak pie. Gregory and Jones looked wistful. Then, with the sudden transitions of boys, Jones caught him by the shoulder. "Look here, Don—know why you're always losing?"

"No." He listened with respect to Jones. Jones always knew things—except the kind of things you learn in school, which he never could learn.

"Well, you haven't got the knack. You put your thumb too far back on the finger. Look here—this is how."

They stooped over the little hole in the roadway, and Jones took Dominic's large hand in his small hand, without appearing to notice its size, and bent the large thumb to the right position on the large finger. "Now try." He tried, and found that the marble had better direction. "I see. I see, Vic. Thanks for the tip."

For some few more minutes they stood talking, arms on each other's shoulders. Then, abruptly as they had met, they parted; and the episode was ended. Jenny was just asking what they should do now, and Gregory and Jones were suggesting a game of egg-cap, when a factory-hooter sent out its melancholy howl. In chorus they said "Hooter. One o'clock," and turned to break up. Dominic too turned; he knew that one o'clock was dinner-time in their homes and his. Gregory and Jones sauntered down the street, looking back to cry "See you after." Jenny slipped into her garden and pulled a marigold, and came to him and stuck it in his coat, with gurgles of laughter. Under the laughing, with her face close to his, she whispered "After school?" He nodded. "Go over the Park—round the Fern Pond?" He nodded and she nodded. They parted in a ballet of conspiratory nods. He saw her slip into her house, and saw the door close on her waving hand. Then, save for three commonplace women, he was alone in that little by-street. Alone, but with dusty trouser-knees, and with a marigold in his coat.

*   *   *   *

He did not remember getting out of the street. The next thing he knew was that he had reached the High Street, and was moving a little unsteadily, and blinking at the speeding traffic. The glowing peace that had enveloped him and filled him while with the children was gone, and he was now aware, not of his earlier depression and fright, but of disturbance; a shake-up of his inner being and of his relations with daily life. He knew that he had in his nature a dark streak of the dreamer, and was sometimes apt to let imagination and fancy play a little wantonly. But he also knew that what had happened had been no prank of imagination or fancy; no trance or dream-state. What had happened had happened as definitely and as really as the passing of those motor-buses and taxis. The children had been there, and they had been real; and they were there now. He could see them, he was sure, again. Though perhaps nobody else could.

He realized that he had been visited by an Experience; something that had never before visited his sober life. But that was all he did know. Neither imagination nor fancy could suggest why he should have had this particular Experience just now. He had met none of the other people he had known in those days—not his mother, or Jenny's mother, or Mrs. Johnson, or the schoolteachers. Only those three. But he had had the Experience. There was the marigold in his coat, and he could still feel the bump on the arm which Jenny's head had given him.

They had all gone in to their dinner, but he did not go to his dinner, or to his lunch. He forgot the Palermo appointment; forgot everything save his mental chaos. He was just able to retain enough control to recognize that it was chaos.

He lifted his stick to an empty taxi, and ordered the driver to Westminster. At a Westminster garage he hired a car. "Drive into the country. What? Oh, anywhere you like, so long as it's the country."

Once out of London, with the car open, and trees and fields and hills and sky about him, his mind cooled. He did not try to think out his adventure; he lay back in the car and brooded upon it. Underneath the disturbance he was aware of a little thrill of delight. The figure of Jenny, and her chatter, remained close to him and held an aroma of—of what? Violets? Daffodils? Hawthorn? The image of London, and of the Palermo and its dining-room and grill-room, and of the solid, adult people who lived there or lunched there, came to him distastefully. Thrusting themselves into his mind, also distastefully, came the people he would have to see to-morrow—City people, who took him seriously as a business-man. He half-wished that they could have seen him playing marbles.

Brooding upon Jenny and the boys, he began to see that the ache of which for many years he had been conscious, and of which many middle-aged men are conscious, was simply an unappeased desire to return to the point where the thread of childhood's other-world had been snapped. By some grace he had been allowed, just for an hour, to return.

He did not notice where the car was going or in what county they were. He noticed only green-hedged lanes and high downs and skies and rushing air, and it was not until he realized that these things had been around him for some long time that he looked at his watch. Five o'clock. By force of habit, the sight of five o'clock on his watch told him that he needed tea, and he took up the speaking-tube and directed the chauffeur to stop at the next decent-looking inn.

After passing two or three at which the chauffeur shook his head, they stopped at a trim little place on a river-bank. "You'll find this all right, sir." He entered the inn's little lounge, gave an order to the landlord for tea, and for the chauffeur's tea, and sat down by the window. The landlord bustled out and within a few seconds bustled back.

"Seen to-day's paper, sir?"

"No. . . . Thanks very much." It was not true. He had, in fact, seen six papers but had scarcely looked at them. He had seen them in bed, with his early tea, and had glanced at the political article and the foreign page of one of them, and had then decided on his visit to his old suburb, and had tossed the rest aside. He took the paper from the landlord listlessly, and went on staring through the window. But the view from the window was not attractive, and he began idly to look through the paper. It was necessary, before to-morrow, that he should re-adjust himself to

the man he was. It was for this reason that he had taken the car
trip. The paper might be an additional help.

Drinking his tea, he ran his eye down column after column.
The paper was one of the popular sort, with all the popular
features. Without absorbing what he was reading he read the
facetious column; read the Social Gossip column; read the Special Article; and wondered whether anybody else ever read these
things. He turned to the secondary news page and the provincial
reports. For a few seconds he glanced at this as he had glanced
at the other pages, and was about to drop the paper when his
glancing changed to positive attention. His eye, as though under
guidance, fell upon three paragraphs in different columns of the
page. It ignored all the rest of the page and went one—two—
three—to the different points. They brought him from his slack,
lounging attitude, and made him sit upright. His casual interest
became eager. His tea became cold.

He read them one by one, and when he had read them he sat
back again and stared at the flowered wall-paper. He stared motionless for some twenty minutes, and at the end of that time his
disturbance had gone, and he was himself.

He got up, put the paper gently aside, and strolled out to the
passage to settle his bill. The landlord, in taking his money, noted
his quiet smile, and spoke about it in the kitchen. It was the smile
of a man who appeared to like the place and to find it good. The
chauffeur, too, noted it, and returned it.

"Back to the shadows now."

"Beg pardon, sir?"

"Back to the old Palermo."

"Very good, sir."

The paragraphs which had caught his attention were three
small news items. There had been a motor smash in Devon, in
which two people were killed. One of them was a James Gregory,
director of a chemical works. There had been a fatal fire-damp
disaster at a northern colliery. The chief engineer, Victor Jones,
in attempting a rescue, had himself perished. There had been
a climbing disaster in the Alps, which had resulted in the death
of three tourists; among them an Englishwoman, a Miss Jane
Wrenn, school-teacher, of London.

FUNSPOT

Once a month Morton passed that street. The business of the firm for which he worked as a collector took him once a month to an office just beyond the limits of the recent spread of the City; an office which called itself City, but was, indeed, North-East.

To reach that office from the Tube station he had to pass that street, and after passing it once a month for two years he found that it had grown upon him and become part of his imaginative life. Every time he passed it, its name, in conjunction with its dark, dishevelled aspect, struck him as bizarre.

After a while, he was wanting to do something about it. Write a song about it or a paragraph about it, or somehow get it into the news. He wished he knew some newspaper man who could make it known. He wanted to see it in headlines; he thought it would look well—"Funspot Street." It seemed to him to cry for dramatization, and he wished it were possible for him to give it celebrity and immortality.

Funspot Street: he saw it on newspaper bills and he heard the radio announcer mentioning it in news-bulletins, and heard the giggles which the name would arouse in a million homes.

He wondered sometimes why it never had been in the news. It was surely made for it. By the look of it it was the sort of street whose people would be fairly regular guests of the police courts, and whose name, when they gave it as an address, would give great chances to the men who write those facetious stories about other people's troubles, which have taken the place of serious police court reporting.

Constantly thinking about it, and seeing it in many connections, comic and dramatic, he decided finally that it would look most apt in type as:—

THE FUNSPOT STREET MURDER.

He could see the sub-heads and cross-heads. Shocking Murder in Funspot Street. . . . Early this morning the police were called to a house in Funspot Street. . . . Detectives working on the Funspot Street tragedy are in possession of an important clue which is likely. . . . Funspot Tragedy Arrest. . . . No Reprieve for Funspot Murderer. . . . And so on.

No; comedy wouldn't do. It called for tragedy, and the more squalid and grotesque the tragedy the more fitting. Something out of the inkwell of Baudelaire or Poe, or De Nerval. He could half-see the kind of thing that would fit, and on each monthly visit to that district the fascination of the name and of fitting it with the right story provided him with entertainment for several evenings. He would add extra details to the half-formed idea in his mind, discarding those of last week in favour of some with a keener edge of the bizarre.

He wasn't a writer, and found it difficult to write two paragraphs in sequence, but the name of that street became almost a muse to him; a spur to do what he couldn't do, and write it into prominence.

He never did write it; but after long brooding there came a time when Funspot Street and its Horrible Tragedy were so clear in his mind that in abstracted moments he could hardly believe that it hadn't happened.

He could locate the house, the room, the time (it would be midnight, of course), and he could visualize the act itself as though he had been an eye-witness. He could see the room and its flimsy, shabby furniture. He could smell the stale, unopened reek of it. He could see the gas-bracket and its incandescent mantle, which would be broken and the flame spluttering.

He could see the violently flowered wallpaper, discoloured in places, and elsewhere peeling off. He could see the strip of cheap carpet, with holes at the points where feet had constantly rested. And he could see the man who had somehow, by some aberration, got into this squalid hole, away from his regular, decent surroundings.

A slim, neatly-dressed fellow, something like himself. And he could see the blowsy woman, the fitting chatelaine of such a house. He could hear the violent noises, and he could see the man turning in fury and disgust and striking the woman and rushing from the room.

And then the mid-day papers, with Funspot Street front-paged. And then the daily and hourly hunt for this decent young chap, just as it might be himself, who, for all his previous decency and integrity, would leave his name in certain records, and be exhibited at Madame Tussaud's as "The Funspot Street Murderer." Not even complete tragedy to mark his sudden fall, but tragedy streaked with the ridiculous. . . . Funspot Street.

In building the story he attributed to the man, at the moment of walking to the scaffold, a burning grievance. Not at his fate, not at the irresponsible moment which had led him to his fate, nor at his capture, when many men who have committed that act have escaped capture. But at the fact that it didn't happen in some other street—in Cavendish Street or Jermyn Street or Kingsway. Over-riding remorse and resignation and the natural horror of the situation would stand this crowning indignity to a man's *finis* —Funspot Street. He felt that it was a good story, if only he could write it.

The salary which his firm considered an adequate balance to the services he rendered did not permit him much evening entertainment; a theatre or music-hall once a month, perhaps, and the movies once a week. Other evenings he spent in wandering about London, getting for nothing an entertainment superior to anything for which one pays money.

On these walks, while observing the pageant, he let his mind play round his Funspot Street Tragedy, going over it again and again, detail for detail. He wished, whimsically, that somebody would put it into action; that there really would be a murder in Funspot Street, just like that, and that the evening paper contents bills would flash it at him. But they never did.

It was on one of these walks, when he was wandering round the strange, lost byways of Islington, and playing with the trial in the Funspot Street Tragedy, and the duel between prisoner and counsel, that something thick touched him softly on the forehead. For one moment he was aware that he was looking closely at a puddle in the road, and that above his head was the number-plate of a taxi and the wheels of a motor-bus. He was aware also of disturbed voices, and then of a babble; and then, through the babble, a firm voice which said: "All right ... we know him ... we'll look after him."

That was all he heard in that moment. Next moment, it seemed, he heard a voice saying, in a low growl: "See if he's got the day's collection on him." And then another voice saying: "'M. Here it is."

His eyelids seemed of iron, but he managed to open them. They gave his eyes a sight of a strip of cheap carpet, with holes here and there. Above him he saw a gas-bracket, with the flame spluttering. Then he saw a violently flowered wallpaper, and places where it was peeling off.

Over him stood a large, heavy man. Just behind the man stood a blowsy woman wearing a flashy, stained frock which he thought he had seen before. In the woman's hands was a bundle of Treasury notes secured with a rubber band.

At the sight of them, and the memory of the words he had heard, his brain began to move. He realized that he had been robbed. The other details passed back into dream, but the fact that he had been robbed remained as a fact. Somehow or other he managed to scramble to his feet and to make a fierce lunge at the woman.

The mid-day papers of next afternoon had Funspot Street well on their bills and on their front pages. But Morton never saw them. The last thing he saw was a poker in the hand of the blowsy woman.

UNCLE EZEKIEL'S LONG SIGHT

Uncle Ezekiel was one of those domestic pests which may be found in thousands of the humbler English homes. The well-to-do have means of parking their Uncle Ezekiels elsewhere; poorer people have to suffer them. These pests sit most of the day and all the evening by the fire. They smoke; they eat; they doze; they grumble; and they monopolize the armchair. They have their little "ways" which they expect everybody to humour, and they make irritating old-man noises. They are seldom beautiful and generally useless; but they are profuse in their criticism of those about them, particularly the young.

This Uncle Ezekiel, pest of a little home in a little South London street, matched all other Uncle Ezekiels save in one minor detail. He was useful. Not until the last year of his life did anybody discover that he was useful, but when it was discovered, this bent and snappy old figure changed the lives of many people of whom he had never heard.

The discovery was made by the lodger of the house, who sometimes came down and talked to the old man, not because he liked him but because he liked talking. Uncle Ezekiel's name for him was "that —— broadcaster," but he only merited the contempt of that term because he was a young man of some crude power which just then expressed itself in talk. After discovering Uncle Ezekiel's usefulness he expressed his power in other directions.

One Friday evening, while making bright conversation, he remarked that the home team were playing at Bemmerton, where they'd never been lucky. Uncle Ezekiel, whose nose was in his beard, and whose eyes were closed, said, "Ar. But they will be this time. They'll have a big win—Five-One."

"Five-One? But they haven't got an earthly. Ford's outa the team, Harper's got a bad knee, and there's a new man being tried out, and——"

"Don't contradict me! I'm old enough to be ya grandfather. But I'm glad I'm not. Tell ya, they'll win Five-One. And Harper'll get four o' the goals. You young chaps think ya know everything."

"But how could they win against the team the others are putting up? And how could Harper——"

Uncle Ezekiel woke up then. "Eh?"

"How could Harper get those goals?"

"Who's Harper?"

"Why—Harper. What we're talking about."

"What *were* we talking about?"

"About the match to-morrer."

"Were we? Where's me terbakker? Someone's always hiding me terbakker."

"Here it is, Uncle. But about the match——"

"Oh——the match. Can't ya talk about anything but football?"

Freddie Pantrome tactfully changed the subject and forgot the old man's ridiculous forecast. But at five o'clock the next afternoon he recalled it. From the evening paper he learned that their team had won 5–1, and that four of the goals had been scored by Harper.

At first he only realized that the old man had been right; it was not until he pondered the matter that he saw its full significance. Since he had been right once, in such detail, was it possible that he might be right again? If so, this threw open a wide door to Mr. Pantrome. Old men—and old women, too—were queer. They were less cluttered with the things of this world. It did happen sometimes that they could see things. He resolved to test it. There was an important re-play on Monday afternoon, and it looked a fairly even match; nothing to choose between the teams.

On Sunday evening, when Uncle Ezekiel was dozing in the best chair and the best corner, he brought up the matter. "Big match to-morrow, Uncle. Starlings playing Nightingales. What hopes!"

Uncle Ezekiel growled, "Starlings'll win. Four-None."

"Four-None? Starlings couldn't do that against——"

"Tell ya Starlings'll win. Don't contradict. Nasty habit you've got——"

Next day Freddie had a busy dinner-hour. He left the engineering yard where he worked, and ran to the post-office to draw two pounds from his savings. It was a big risk, but Freddie knew that big men only got through by taking big risks. With the two pounds he sought out five or six of the bookmakers' runners, and laid out five shillings here, five shillings there, five shillings with another, and ten shillings with the most important.

At half-past four that afternoon he tried to tell himself that it was just a bit of fun, and that really there was nothing to it. But the greater part of himself was listening for the newsboy, and when he heard that voice he shot out to the gate, and grabbed a paper from the boy. "Football Results—Starlings v. Nightingales (re-play), Starlings 4, Nightingales 0." He had grabbed the paper before handing the penny. Having read the result, he passed six-pence to the boy and waved him on. The boy stared; turned the sixpence over twice; bit it; then graciously permitted himself to be waved on.

That evening Freddie owned seven pounds more than he had owned in the morning. And he began to ponder the enigma of Uncle Ezekiel even more deeply. He wondered whether his powers centred solely on football, or whether they could be ap-plied to other things. He resolved on another test. Newmarket was opening on Wednesday. Racing had never much interested him, but next day he bought all the sporting papers, and studied, not form, but prices.

Having noted the runners, notably those of long price, he went downstairs and kindly entertained Uncle Ezekiel by reading to him about the building strike. He went on reading until Uncle Ezekiel dozed off, which was achieved in two paragraphs. Fred-die's voice, in a confined space, was grey grit, but full of lights and inflexions in yards and other open spaces. Then he said, "Wonder what'll win the Big Race to-morrow, Uncle. What do *you* think?"

"Think?" Uncle growled from his beard. "I don't think. I *know*. Ice Cream Cornet."

"Ice Cre—— Why, it's thirty-three to one to-night."

"I can't help that. It's goin' ta win. Don't take up everything I say, like that. I know more'n you."

"I admit that, Uncle. You certainly do. I wonder what'll do the four o'clock."

"The four o'clock. That'll be the one carrying the little feller with the moustache. Can't think of his name."

"That'll be Trollope. Riding Ampersand. Sixty-six to one. And if you say it'll win, Uncle, of course it will. What a nice surprise for some of 'em."

Freddie was still not accepting Uncle in full faith, but he decided to play with five pounds of his seven, and if it went he would still have two pounds more than he had last week. Next day he did not consult the runners. He went to the offices of the local bookmakers. He laid a pound with two of them on Ice Cream Cornet. With a third (and larger) establishment he laid a pound on Ice Cream Cornet; all winnings on Ampersand. With a fourth he laid two pounds on Ampersand.

On the following Monday he collected four figures. His first dealings with his wealth were to buy Uncle Ezekiel a case of whisky and a hundred cigars. Uncle Ezekiel looked at the whisky and smelt the cigars, and said, "What's this for?"

Freddie said, "It's for you."

"Why? You come into money, or something?"

"In a way, yes. You gave me the winners of two races, Tuesday of last week. And I backed 'em."

"Winners of two races? Did I?"

"Course you did. Don't you remember?"

"I don't. You was talking about the building strike last Toosday. Lot o' rot you was talking, too. Still, if you say I did, I s'pose I did. I always take people's word. I never contradict. S'pose you make ye'self useful fer once, an' open one o' those bottles."

That was the beginning of the founding of the fortune of Mr. Frederic Pantrome. His natural kindness in talking to a lonely and craggy-tempered old man, though it derived from his equally natural love of hearing his own voice, brought results which these things seldom bring. He cast his bread upon the waters and it came back spread with caviare.

In Uncle Ezekiel he had found the gate to an Eldorado, and the Open Sesame for this gate was as simple a business as lighting a cigarette. When he wanted advance information, all he had to do was to read to the old man until he got him dozing, and then shoot the question. The answer came automatically—and always correctly.

Two months after that first football match, Freddie had an office of his own and rooms on the other side of the bridges in Southampton Row. He was no fool. Easy money did not mean to him easy living and fatuous luxury. It meant an opening to interesting work and a variety of operations in the world of mechanical invention. He continued to be a visitor, twice a week, to the little house in the side street, and he continued to talk and read to Uncle Ezekiel. On the Cesarewitch and Cambridgeshire he became, by Uncle Ezekiel's unaware help, independent for life. With twelve different bookmakers he placed bets varying from fifty pounds to a hundred pounds on the double, and had only to wait until the second race was run. The first was won by a favourite; the second by an outsider.

With a few more ventures of this kind, and two Stock Exchange speculations, on which Uncle's advice was totally against the market, his money grew and grew—as money will grow, once you have enough of it. Towards the end of the year he had so much that it ceased to interest him, and he no longer needed Uncle's help for himself. He used it for the benefit of his friends, and for discovering which inventions were worth backing.

The odd thing was that nobody else could get anything out of Uncle Ezekiel. Freddie did not, of course, disclose the source of what his friends called his infernal luck, and his enemies, of whom he had made a few, grudgingly called his remarkable judgment of the course of affairs. He never mentioned Uncle Ezekiel or any other uncle. But neither Uncle Ezekiel's niece, nor her husband, could get anything out of him. They had seen the results in Freddie's case, and received benefit from it, but they couldn't do it themselves. They couldn't get him dozing. It was only Freddie's flat, arid tones that could produce the right kind of doze. Not that they needed to do it, for Freddie had recognized that his fortune had come from that little house, and he was handing back to them as much as they wanted of it.

During the last year of his life Uncle Ezekiel could have wallowed in luxury, had he been the wallowing kind. But the critical attitude suited him better than the acceptant, and Freddie and

Freddie's visits were still received with something short of approval.

"Well, what y'inventing now? Something to make life more difficult, I s'pose. What's that you brought? Oysters? Grrr.... Now you got up in this fancy world you got all these fancy notions. I 'ate shell-fish. Ain't you 'eard me say dozens o' times that what I like is a good steak-and-kidney pudden? Not the kind that fool of a niece o' mine makes, but a real one. And then you bring me oysters. And last time it was pheasant. Don't I deserve any consideration? You keep saying it was my advice what made you. And well it might be. If more young people'd listen to their elders what've 'ad more experience of life. But if it was, why don't ya do something about it? These 'ere cigars. You say they run to half a crown apiece. More fool you. Most of 'em I gave away. What I like is a good *smoking* terbakker. Try and remember that. But I never can get what I want. This dam-fool chair you bought me. All these dam-fool tricks fer raising it and shifting the back. Why couldn't ya get me a sensible chair?"

"All right, Uncle Ezekiel. I'll have it taken away and get you a really——"

"Who said I wonnid it taken away? I like it. To look at. You can send me summan else to sit in."

"You do love complaining, don't you, Uncle?"

"What if I do? I bin complained at by other people most o' me life. Time I did a bit fer meself."

"All right.... By the way, d'you know what happened last week?"

"Course I do. I read the papers, don't I?"

"I mean to me. Two things. I was interviewed by the Press about that new aero engine I'm backing—for a 'plane that'll fit round a man's body. And I met the most wonderful girl in the world."

"You would. Any young feller with as much money as you got couldn't 'elp meeting 'er. Or being met by 'er. I thought you was the one sensible young feller there was. My mistake."

Freddie ignored this remark. Uncle Ezekiel was awake, and was speaking from his own restricted mind. He was valuable only when he was half-asleep. Freddie went on talking about his engine. ". . . .What it means is that if you want to go from London to Paris, you just go. You just take off from your own front door. If we can get it right, people in this street could have 'em. Just take off from here and go anywhere they wanted to go. Margate, Egypt, Persia—anywhere. And the whole contraption no bigger than a suit-case. The big feature about the thing—a bit of blind genius in the chap whose idea it is—is the elimination of——"

Uncle Ezekiel's nose was sinking deeper into his beard. Freddie noted this and ran on from "elimination" to "Olive." "Olive's frightfully keen on it. She's the daughter of a big man I've been dealing with. Clever girl. She understands things. We get on jolly well together. She wanted to make the first experimental flight in the thing, but I won't let her. Too risky."

Uncle Ezekiel growled from his beard. "No risk. It'll be all right."

"Will it?"

"Ar. Safe as anything else. You'll make a Do with that thing."

"I hope so. Because Olive's so keen on it. She's a wonderful girl. I wonder if she really cares for me."

"Course she does. And just the girl fer you, too. This time next year you'll know that."

"How shall I know it?"

" 'Cos you'll be married to 'er, o' course."

Freddie smacked the table and said "Ha!" Uncle Ezekiel woke up with the smack. "Wodya making all this noise for? You always was noisy, Freddie, when you was living 'ere. Banging about, just when I was 'aving forty winks. You know 'ow bad I sleep. And that reminds me. Don't go giving that fool of a niece of mine any more money. Nor Joe. You already given 'em more'n they know what to do with. There's 'er getting Lord-knows-what kind o' dresses. And now talking about moving to a larger 'ouse. And about buying me a cottage t'meself and a woman to look after me. Nice upset that'd be fer me, wouldn't it? 'Ave a bit o' consideration."

"But I must give them something. I got my fortune from this house—from you—and everybody ought to share it."

"That's all right and proper. But don't give 'em money. People oughtn't t'ave money till they're old. Then they're sensible enough to realize it ain't worth 'aving."

★

Nearly a year after that first football bet, Freddie sat with Olive in a restaurant in Jermyn Street—one of the four quiet and band-less restaurants remaining in London. They were celebrating the successful trial of the new Everybody's 'Plane.

Freddie, who now had a flat in Pall Mall, was almost unrecognizable from the crude young man who had made those football bets. It was not that his outward appearance had changed so much as his whole bearing. It was not that he was wearing fine clothes, but the way he was wearing them. He did not carry his prosperity with any show of swagger, or any awkwardness. To his native force he had added poise, and he carried his success as something he had always known and taken for granted. He treated money as though he had always had it, and he stepped into this new mode of life as an exile returning to his true home. His voice had lost its flat tone; it was not so easy for him, as it had been, to send Uncle Ezekiel into a doze.

During dinner, the subject of Uncle Ezekiel came up; not by name but by reference. "By the way," Olive said; "you've told me once or twice about a queer old friend you've got. Some labouring man living in South London who advises you. Who gets knowledge of what's going to happen. Those winners you gave young Jack—I think you said *they* came from him."

"They did. And everything else I've got."

"Sounds hardly believable, but if you say so, it must be so. I've heard you say you put complete faith in anything he says."

"I do. He's always right."

" 'M. . . . He'd be useful to a government if there was any trouble breaking in Europe, and they wanted to know which group to back. But I suppose they wouldn't pay any attention to him."

"I've thought of that. He *would* be useful. And I'm giving him every attention he can need to keep him with us. In case of anything like that. And if they laughed at the idea, I think I could soon convince them with a few immediate things—like to-morrow's winners, and what they'd win by; and what price any given stock would be at four o'clock any afternoon."

"Well, I wonder if he could do something for me."

"Anything you like. What is it?"

"I know it sounds silly, but. . . . It's about Dad. You know he's sailing for America on Wednesday. On the new boat. Its maiden voyage. Well, I've got a feeling about that boat. Not because they started work on it on the thirteenth, and it's sailing for the first time on Friday, but . . . some other feeling. I wonder if you could find out from him if it's all right."

"Sure. Let's see. It's Friday. I'll see him on Sunday evening, and give you a ring."

On Sunday evening Freddie found it difficult to get Uncle Ezekiel off. He wanted to talk about his niece's objectionable behaviour with money. He wanted to talk about the boy next door who was learning the clarinet. But by a determined insistence on the state of affairs in the Near East, and frequent references to "sanctions" and "plebiscites," Freddie finally got him off. It was hard going, but he stuck to it.

"Well, what's the best news *you* got?"

"The best news? I'm not sure. But the most interesting, I think, is the situation in the Near East."

"Near East me big toe. Don't y'ever 'ear any new risky stories? Mixing wi' the best people, as you do, y'ought tuv picked up a few by now."

"I'm afraid I've been too busy."

"Ar. You'll learn better one o' these days. You'll learn that yer own fireside's more important than any Near East or any other bit o' the compass."

"But you'd find it really interesting if you'd let me explain. You see, it's like this. The territory set aside by the treaty——"

Uncle Ezekiel turned his back. Freddie droned on. He droned until he saw that Uncle was nodding. Then he broke a sentence to ask, "What about the *Panwangler*, Uncle? Making its maiden voyage on Wednesday. Friend of mine's sailing on it. My future father-in-law, I hope. Olive's father, Mr. Dreamersdew."

"Eh?" Momentarily he came out of his doze.

"The *Panwangler*. Making its maiden voyage on Wednesday. Mr. Dreamersdew's sailing on it."

"Oodya say?"

"Mr. Dreamersdew. I was wondering if it'd have a good voyage."

"Mr. Dreamersdew. 'M . . . Dreamersdew . . . *Panwangler*. . . ."

For some seconds he seemed completely asleep. Freddie had to recall him.

"Well, Uncle, what about the *Panwangler?*"

"*Panwangler's* all right. Good ship."

"Will Mr. Dreamersdew do any good business in New York?"

"Mr. Dreamersdew'll do a lot in New York."

"I'm glad to hear that. He was hesitating about going."

Uncle Ezekiel jerked his head, opened his eyes, and puffed. "Wassat? Talking about going? Well, yer 'at's on the sideboard. Nothing stopping ya that I know of."

Four evenings later Freddie stood in front of Uncle Ezekiel, holding a newspaper to him. Or perhaps, so threatening was the manner, *at* him. "Look at that. Look at it." He was cold and stern. He knew that he had no right to be angry with Uncle Ezekiel, but he *was* angry. "Olive's father. They trusted me. I trusted you. I told them it was safe for him to go. And now look at that."

"That" was a report of the sinking of the *Panwangler.* The list of sixteen survivors did not carry the name Dreamersdew. "Olive'll never forgive me." He looked down at Uncle Ezekiel who was blinking at the page of the newspaper. "What was the matter with you Sunday night? How did it happen? You've never been wrong before about anything. How did you come to be wrong about this?"

Uncle Ezekiel mumbled and chewed his pipe-stem. "I dunno. P'r'aps it was because I was thinking. I can always do it better if I don't think."

Freddie dropped the paper and gave a large sigh. He stared at the wall of the little kitchen, and moved his feet nervously. "Why did I ask you? Why didn't I leave it alone? Olive couldn't have blamed me then. She'll feel now. . . ." He took the two paces which was all the tiny room allowed for a walk, and stared at a grocer's almanack.

He was still staring at it when he was aware of a queer noise in the room. He looked round to locate it; first on the floor; then at the fire. Then he found its true source. Uncle Ezekiel was laughing. He turned on him with: "Dammit, man, what on earth are you laughing about? Haven't you got any feelings? A thing like this—and you laugh. . . ."

Uncle Ezekiel coughed and choked. "Sorry. I was laughing at me being wrong. All through thinking. I got it right about the *Panwangler* when you first mentioned it. I saw it. And then I woke up and got thinking. Thinking of Dreamersdew. When I was caretaker at 'is place. Thinking of the time when the missus was on her dying bed. And wanting things. And 'e turned me off 'cos I answered back when 'e called me a Useless Ole Slacker."

Late that night Uncle Ezekiel died in his chair. The family were surprised; they had thought he was looking so well lately. They didn't know that it was the necessary and inevitable full-stop to one who had misused a great gift for selfish revenge.

THE HORRIBLE GOD

Mr. Rainwater wasn't easily scared, but for the last three or four days he had had a strong feeling that he was being followed, and it was upsetting him. He knew that the feeling of being followed is often a symptom of a neurotic or morbid state, but that wasn't his state. He was quite healthy, and free of melodramatic or nervous imaginings. He was being followed. He could feel it through his skin. He could feel it in the air the moment he left his home. He could feel pursuit and the prickings of danger.

Towards midnight that evening his suspicion became certainty. He was walking down Shaftesbury Avenue towards Piccadilly and was in the thick of the crowd coming from the theatres when, clearly and with electrical urgency, a voice reached his ear. It was a keen mutter, and it said: "I speak as a friend. The vengeance of the god Imbrolu is a terrible vengeance. He seeks his own place."

Rainwater turned swiftly. He collided with two girls just behind him who were giggling and talking of Ronald Colman. On one side of him a policeman was striding. On the other side was a wall. Two paces ahead was a newsboy, and walking away from him were a couple of nondescript youths who had evidently been drinking.

As the crowd swirled round him he looked here and there for the possible speaker, but could see nobody to whom that queer mutter could have belonged. It was not an English mutter.

On the opposite side of the street was a large negro in a brilliant blue suit; in a bus coming from Piccadilly Circus sat a man of muddy colour and Oriental features; and outside the Monico, some 30 yards away, was an Algerian rug-seller. But the distance of these men from him made it impossible for any of them to have spoken those words in his ear two seconds ago.

He stood and considered. It was odd; very odd. The voice had been so sharp and so close that it must have been addressing him. It had come right into his ear, as though the mouth had been touching his shoulder. Yet nobody to whom he could trace it. He knew, of course, the trick of self-effacement; that sleek movement by which a cat will pass round you before your eyes without your seeing it, and which certain people can achieve by a cessation of mental action. He attributed the vanishing of the speaker to that, and he had reason for believing that the speaker was not English. The message, he was sure, was meant for him, and no other person in the crowd; he was sure that it connected with his feeling of being followed, and that everything connected with that horrible idol.

The idol had been worrying Rainwater for some time—even before the following had begun. It was an idol of a kind he had never before seen; an idol which gave him the shudders every time he looked at it. As a collector of native bric-à-brac, he was accustomed, even hardened, to the many variations upon certain themes of which the black mind, in its more exalted fervours, is capable.

But this. . . . The most cloistered nun, knowing nothing of the images by which men express the baseness of man, would have known at a glance that this thing was in form and spirit horrible. The most experienced Madame of a Buenos Aires sailors' hotel would not have confused it with the realistic emblems of native religions which her customers brought from their voyages and with which they improved her knowledge of anthropology. It was just a masterpiece of unrelated horror.

The artist who made it had withdrawn from the unfenced fields of religious ardour and had immured himself within the narrow dogmas of art—just to show, apparently, that art, with all its fetters of form and technique, could outsoar anything achieved under the licence and tolerance by which the darker religions distinguish themselves from art.

Certainly he had succeeded. Never had Rainwater, under that cloak of respectability which hides so many anomalies, even imagined anything like it. Nor had anybody else whom he knew. Of all his acquaintances among curators of museums, not one could put a name to it or even conjecture the country or island of its origin. When he showed it to them they stared and whistled.

And that was all he could get from them. They could tell him that it wasn't Egypt, that it wasn't Java, that it wasn't Easter Island, or Haiti, or Liberia; but they couldn't tell him what it *was*. They could only tell him that he'd better put it away or throw it away.

He put it away at the bottom of one of his curio cabinets. He couldn't give it away, because nobody he knew would have accepted it. All his friends were married. And as a collector he couldn't bring himself to throw it away. Yet, in keeping it in his rooms, he felt a distinct unease, as though in possessing it he were partly responsible for its horror and had had a share in making it.

He *wanted* to throw it away, or burn it, or drop it over one of the bridges, but whenever he reached the point of setting out to do it, the collecting instinct mastered him. If the thing had been emitting an evil smell into his room he still wouldn't have been able to screw himself up to throwing it away. So he kept it locked up, and only took it out now and then, which made him feel more guilty.

If a friend was announced he would hurriedly hide it. If he heard his housekeeper's step outside the door he would throw a newspaper over it. When he had had it for three weeks his demeanour had become almost furtive.

And then began that feeling of being followed and its climax of that muttered message. He wished he had never seen the wretched thing, or, having seen it, had resisted the temptation to buy it. The thing itself was a horror and now it was leading to this uncanny following and this uncanny message delivered in a crowded street. He didn't know what to do about it.

It wasn't the threat that disturbed him so much as the stealthy following and the manner in which the threat had been delivered. If it was the ju-ju of some tribe or creed with representatives in London why couldn't they come to him openly? Why the following about, which had begun apparently from the moment he bought it, when he had been followed to his home? And how could he put the little hideous god back in his own place when nobody, not even scholars, knew whence it came?

He walked on in some disturbance. Every now and then he looked back or stopped by a shop whose side-window reflected the path behind him, but he saw nobody who might be the follower, and did not expect to. Whoever had been following him the last few days was an experienced shadower; clever enough to convey the horrid sense of his neighbourhood and clever enough to remain unperceived.

Mr. Rainwater was beginning to realize that there is something in being followed which is more shocking than a revolver at the head or a knife at the throat. There is nothing to grasp; nothing to combat; only a persistent nagging at the nerves, which in time can wear you down.

And Rainwater was being worn down. If they wanted their god they could have it, so far as he was concerned. He couldn't throw an artistic treasure away, but if it meant something more to people than it did to him they were welcome to it, if only they would come and ask for it. They must know his address or they wouldn't be able to follow him as they did. Why, then, this menacing and muttering of vengeance?

On reaching home he learned that they did know his address. His housekeeper met him in the hall. She held a grubby piece of pink paper. "I don't know what this is, sir, or how it came. I found it on the mat under the evening paper. Would it be anything you know about?" She passed it to him. It bore six words in an ungainly scrawl: "Imbrolu waits. You have been warned."

Mr. Rainwater made a noise of irritation.

He passed it back to her. "No, I don't know anything about it. Some odd bit of waste paper that blew in, I should think." But he went upstairs feeling a little sick. When he got to his room he went first to the little cabinet in which he kept the horrible thing.

The room was filled with the results of his collecting mania. They hung on the walls, they stood on tables and they decorated half a dozen glass cabinets; tribal work mainly, all of it bizarre. The horrible thing was not resting in one of the glass cabinets. It was in an old lacquer cabinet—a nest of drawers three times concealed within other drawers. He had just opened it and had reached the drawer containing the thing when, without conscious impulse, he went to the window and moved the curtain aside. He moved it aside casually; he dropped it swiftly.

On the opposite pavement under the overhanging trees of a front garden, was a motionless figure. The figure was dressed in a raincoat, and its soft hat had the brim turned down. To see the face was impossible, but something about the pose of the figure conveyed to Mr. Rainwater the sense of alien ideas. He turned from the window, shut all the drawers and doors of the cabinet, without looking to see if his treasure was there, and dropped into a chair by the fire.

He had scarcely dropped when he got up again; found a glass; mixed himself a drink. He went back to the chair with it, and dropped again. He wasn't a coward and he wasn't a man of stout nerve. He was like most of us, in between, and ready to admit when he was shaken. He was a mild and amiable man, but could, as mild and amiable people can, be capable of ferocity when really roused and when there was some concrete object of his ferocity.

Such as a man who insisted on having the window of a railway carriage closed on a warm day.

But against intangible hostility, or against anything unfamiliar, he was a reed. His heart didn't give way, but his nerves did. None of the incidents of the last four days had made him afraid, but they had brought him to the edge of a breakdown. He needed a drink.

Sitting there in the midnight silence he began to hear, or to think he could hear, odd noises from the street. Little soft noises, of the kind that make people ask each other in whispers—"What's that?" Once or twice, without knowing why, he looked over at the lacquer cabinet, and found himself relieved to see that it was still there and still a lacquer cabinet.

He wanted to go to the window again, but couldn't. He wanted to know if the figure had gone, but there was the possibility that he would see it standing in the same position; and he didn't want to see it. There was nothing in the figure itself, or in its attitude, to disturb anyone: it was just a solitary and motionless man. Yet its mere presence conveyed a stream of menace and portent and alarm which was the more potent for being obscure.

It created that shrinking of the skin which man always knows before the nameless peril. In its immobility it was horrid, and Mr. Rainwater didn't want to see it. Also, he had a feeling that, horrid as it was in stillness, it would fill him with more horror if it moved.

He wanted to go to bed, but couldn't. He had half an idea of taking the horrible idol from the cabinet, opening the window, and flinging it out to the watcher. But if it fell in the roadway it might smash, and that might mean more of this furtive persecution. And he felt that he couldn't stand much more of it. He was accustomed to a peaceful life, and he could not adjust himself to this invasion of his peace.

Somehow or other he must get rid of the thing. He couldn't give it to a museum, because that might bring persecution on the museum's curator, and if he burnt it or dropped it in the river, he still wouldn't be free of their attentions. And he couldn't hand it over to them because they never came near enough to him. If he took it out now, and went downstairs to give it to the solitary watcher, he was certain that the solitary watcher would have vanished.

But about three o'clock in the morning, after his third drink, which had done his nerves three times no-good, an idea came to him. A simple idea which should have come to him when the persecution began. He would pass it to the people most able to deal with the situation. He would resell it to the shop where he bought it, at any price they cared to give. It was a dim little shop, kept by two swarthy old men who looked as though they could understand and answer any roundabout messages.

On that resolution he went to bed, not caring whether the house was surrounded, or whether he was to be burgled or assassinated, or not. He was beyond caring. His nerves had jittered so much under the persecution, and had developed such a side-jittering from the three heavy drinks, that they were now exhausted. Anything could happen, but Mr. Rainwater was going to bed.

Nothing did happen; and after a miniature breakfast he took the horrible god from the private drawer of the cabinet, packed it carefully in tissue-paper, put it into his overcoat pocket, and set out for the shop, followed, he was sure, all the way.

He did not get rid of it so easily as he had hoped. The partners were not in a buying mood. When he offered it, saying that he was tired of it, and that it was not in keeping with the rest of his collection, they hesitated. They answered as curio-dealers always do; they did not want it. Those things, they said, were not easy to sell. When they could sell that kind of thing they got a good price, but they might have to keep it in stock for a year, two years, five years, before finding a customer. They had had it in stock for three years before Mr. Rainwater bought it.

Mr. Rainwater asked: would they make an offer? They replied that they would hardly dare. The offer would be too ridiculous. They really did not want it; the small demand for such things made it impossible to offer a price at all relative to the artistic value of the thing.

Mr. Rainwater said sternly: "Name a price."

Under compulsion they named, with confusion and apology, ten shillings.

"I'll take it." He pushed the horrible god across the counter. They tendered, across the counter, sadly and with deprecation, a ten-shilling note. He took it; said "Good morning"; and walked out into the morning sun.

Outside, he took a deep breath, said, "That's that, thank God," and walked away as though liberated from clanking chains. He walked all the way to his club, and did not once have the feeling of being followed. This restoration of his normal life filled him with the holiday spirit, and he spent the ten shillings, and more, in a super-excellent lunch.

*   *   *   *

That evening, in the little shop the partners smiled at each other. "Yes," said one, "we have done well with this thing which the English sailor carved for us. Eight times we have sold it; and eight times we have frightened the buyer into bringing it back." In a mocking sing-song he recited: "The vengeance of the god Imbrolu is a terrible vengeance. He seeks his own place. . . . These superstitious English!"

FATHER AND SON

Sam was hard-up; and when Sam was hard-up the very few scruples that composed the trifle which served him as conscience got out of the way. He wasn't hard-up as you and I are hard-up; he wanted only a few shillings. But relatively his situation was as acute as yours or mine, and he had none of the instincts and training which enable us to put up with it and wait till things change. He couldn't put up with anything that interfered with his wants.

He wasn't a rogue. He wasn't the kind of lad who, needing a few shillings, would go out with the smash-and-grab or hold-up boys. He was a jellied eel. His face at a passing glance in the street was a normal face, but if you took a long look at it you began to think of something out of the Wiertz Museum. He had no zest for goodness and no guts for evil. All he could be was mean and milky. Mean and milky in his good tendencies and mean and milky in his rebellions.

He was rebelling against circumstance that afternoon, but there was nothing of the Cromwell or Garibaldi in his rebellion. His rebellion took the form, not of knocking things over but of slinking round them. He was looking, as he always did, not for a fight with circumstance, but for an easy way out. He leaned against a lamp-post at the corner, interfering with the sunshine and doing his bit of rebellion. He needed a few shillings, and that trifle told him that he mustn't even think of taking them. That was dangerous. He must justify and protect himself in getting them. He must earn them. He was not delicate as to the manner in which he earned them, but he barred all other ways of getting them, except possibly cadging them, and there was nobody from whom to cadge. So he leaned against the post, blinking and considering how he might earn them.

He wouldn't have had to do any considering if his father had continued to do his duty in the matter of petty cash. But lately his father had Turned Nasty. After being a constant and easy source of supply he had begun to be reluctant in handing out shillings. He had begun to nag. He had told his son what he himself was doing at eighteen. From the tone in which he related this, it appeared that he was dissatisfied with his son. It appeared, too, that he himself had been the exemplar upon which numbers of men who wore honours and owned large balances had modelled their lives. It appeared that Samuel Smiles would have added another chapter to his book had he lived long enough to hear about Sam's father. It appeared, most certainly, that it would be useless to ask the old man for those shillings.

No doubt the old man's friends were responsible for this change of attitude. They had never quite approved of Sam, and when he had made complaints to them concerning the old man and pocket-money, he had won none of their sympathy. They had talked of Regular Work, and of Spongers and Pieces of Wet String. They had spoken of the old man's usual attitude to his son as unduly generous, while admitting that other people would have called it dam-foolish. They had trespassed beyond the bounds of courtesy by foreshadowing his probable fate had he been *their* son. They had left him feeling bad about things.

It was while he was brooding upon their words and upon his problem that he remembered the talk there had lately been about the large amount of tobacco which was going around the neighbourhood. It was going around, too, at such a price that, considering the current duty, only a philanthropist, willing to lose money for the benefit of others, could have sold it at the price. Authority, he knew, was much concerned about this business, and wanted to interview the philanthropist. But it couldn't locate his address, and it was hampered in the search for it by being unable to quote his name.

Sam knew both. And Sam had read stories about men who did the hazardous work of detecting crime without official help, and who served their country quietly and without any desire for lime-light. So, when the bars opened, he left his lamp-post, and went in and deliberated the matter over a lonely half-pint. It looked safe and it looked virtuous. It ought to be done. And it ought to be worth something when done. And it might lead to other things. Small beginnings . . . as his father was always saying.

When he saw the bottom of his glass he came to a decision. He would earn private gratitude, and anything else that might be going, by a virtuous piece of work. He put the glass on the counter, straightened his tie by the mirror, and set out to do it. There would be a girl at the corner to-morrow night. That was the source of his need of shillings. A man must have a few shillings in his pocket when he meets a girl. And he must do his duty as a citizen.

So he went and did it. The man he went to see received him somewhat coldly. But he listened to what Sam had to say, and when various questions brought some long-wanted details, he thawed. He admitted at the end of the interview that Sam had been useful, and he returned the service. Sam went out to the twilit street with the clear mind which comes with a problem solved.

He was waiting at the corner next evening, in full ease of mind, for the encounter with the girl, when a young, alert man came to him.

"You're wanted at the station."

"Who—me?"

"Yes, you. Won't take you a minute. Just an identification."

So he went with the young man, and in the hall of the station he saw one or two officers; two civilians, looking somewhat awkward; and a third civilian sitting meekly on a bench. The third civilian looked up at his son with eyes that registered nothing in particular and little flicks of a dozen different emotions.

One of the officers whispered to Sam: "D'you see here the man you say is doing this tobacco game?"

"'Mm. Sitting on the bench there."

"Ah. What name d'you know him by?"

"Joe Swot."

"Oh. . . . Same name as yours, eh? Any relation?"

"My father."

"Your——" The officer's eyes registered something very particular. "Oh. . . . Really. . . . That's interesting." He looked Sam over. Then he looked at the old man, sitting with drooped hands. Then he looked back at Sam, with an expression which suggested that something in the air had gone sour. "All right. You can go." He put an emphasis on the word "go."

Sam hesitated. He hadn't seen it like this. He didn't like the officer's manner, and he didn't like the hard eyes of the two civilians, and he didn't like the stares of the other officers. This didn't seem a fitting reception to one who was doing his duty. They were all looking at him in a thoroughly offensive manner, as though there were something unpleasant about him. He wanted to ask them about their looks, but as they were still staring at him, and the stares were becoming almost hypnotic, he restrained himself. He turned and slouched out. He slouched so definitely, to show his nonchalance, that he didn't notice the little threshold against which the doors fitted. He caught his foot in it; stumbled; and went headlong down the steps.

Those inside turned to look, and in that moment the old man made a dash for the door. There were cries of "Stop. . . . Hold him. . . . Quick." Two officers sprang after him, but they over-ran themselves. The old man had stopped abruptly in the doorway. He stood there bent, peering down into the half-darkness.

"Hurt yehself, son? Did y'urt yehself?"

JOHNSON LOOKED BACK

Don't look behind you, Johnson. There's a man following you, but don't look behind. Go on just as you are going, down that brown-foggy street where the lamps make diffuse and feeble splashes on the brown. Go straight on and don't look behind, or you might be sorry. You might see something that you'll wish you hadn't seen.

He's a blind man, Johnson, but that makes little difference to him, and is of no use to you. You can't hear the tapping of his stick because he hasn't got a stick. He can't carry a stick. He hasn't any hands. But he's been blind so long that he can walk the streets of this district without a stick. He can smell his way about, and he can feel traffic and other dangers through his skin.

You can turn and twist as you like, and use your mortal eyes as much as you like, but that man without eyes will be close on your trail. He's faster than you. He's not impeded by perception of the objects that reach you through the eyes. You are not used to the uncertain cloud of fog and blears of light; you have to pick your steps. He can march boldly, for he marches always in clear, certain darkness. If you use cunning he can meet all your cunning. Without seeing you, or hearing you, he will know just where you go, and he will be close behind you. He will know what you are going to do the moment you have decided to do it; and he will be at your heels.

No; it won't help you at all to look behind you. It will only sicken you. It's not a pleasant spectacle—this man, blind and without hands, silently and steadfastly dogging you through the curling vapour. It's much better for you not to know that you are being pursued by this creature. The result will be the same anyway; you won't escape him, and it may save you a few minutes of misery not to know what is coming.

But why is he pursuing you? Why did he wait so long at the entrance to that dim street, whose very lamps seem to be ghosts of its darkness, to pick out your step from many others, and to follow you with this wolf-stride? You will not know that until you see him face to face. You have forgotten so many things; things that the strongest effort of memory will not recall, but your pursuer hasn't. He remembers; and all these years he has been seeking you, smelling about the streets of London, knowing that some day he is certain to strike the forbidding street down which you went when you first shook him off, and that he will find you there. And to-night he has found it and has smelt your presence there, and is with you once again.

Purpose is pursuing impulse. You are idle and at ease. He is in ferment. You are going to visit that abandoned house because it occurred to you to visit that abandoned house. He is following you because he has been waiting for nothing else. So there you go—he patient and intent; you, with free mind, picking your steps through the fog-smeared street. You have nothing to worry about. You walk through the fog with care, but with that sense of security which even the darkest streets of London cannot shake in Londoners familiar with them and with their people. You don't know what is catching up with you, and so long as you go straight ahead and don't look——

Oh, you fool! Johnson—you fool! I said—"*Don't* look behind you."

And now you've looked. And now you've seen. And now you know.

If you hadn't looked behind you would have escaped all the years of pain that are now coming upon you. It would have been all over in a few seconds. Now you've made it more dreadful. You've filled your mind with knowledge of it, and you're going to increase your torment by trying to get away. And above those two pains will come the pain of a struggle.

You won't get away. You have no chance at all. The man behind you is blind, and has no hands; but he has arms and he has feet, and he can use them. Don't think you can escape by dodging down that alley. . . . That was a silly thing to do. Alleys hold fear more firmly than open streets. Fear gets clotted in their recesses and hangs there like cobwebs. You thought you were doing something clever which would perplex him, but you won't perplex him. He is driving you where he wants you. You thought that if you could get into the alleys, and twist and turn and double along the deserted wharves, you could shake him off. But you can't. It's just in the alleys that he wants to have you, and you went there under his direction.

Already you're helping him because you're feeling the clotted fear which has been hanging in these alleys through the centuries. You're getting muddled. You've lost count of the turns you've taken, and you're not sure whether you're going away from him or fleeing breast to breast upon him. You saw him in all his maimed ugliness, and you see him now in every moving heap of fog that loiters at the mouth of each new alley. Long before he is upon you, he has got you.

If you hadn't looked back, doom would have fallen upon you out of nothing. But you looked back, and now you know the source of that doom.

You might as well give up padding through the alleys. Their universe of yellow-spotted blackness is only deluding you with hope of refuge. No corner is dark enough to hide you from eyes that live in darkness. No doors can cover you from senses as keen as air. No turn that you take will carry you farther from him; you are taking the turns he wants you to take.

There! You've turned into a little square which has no opening save that by which you entered. You're done. You can't hear him coming because he's wearing thin list slippers; but he's very near you. He's very near that entry. You've no hope of getting out. When he seizes you it would be better to yield everything, cat-like, and go with his desire and his attack. Better that than to fight. Only fools fight the invincible. But of course you *will* fight.

Hush—he's here. He's at the entry. He's in the square. You know that he's moving towards you; you know it as certainly as steel knows magnet. And then, though the fog-filled square gives you no more sight than your enemy, you know that he has halted; and you feel the silence dripping about your ears, spot by spot.

And now he has made his spring. He is upon you, and your fists fly against him. But you cannot beat him back. His blows fall upon you, and they wound and sting. You cannot fight him as you would fight another man. Your blood is cold but your brain is hot, and your nerves and muscles receive confused commands. They begin to act by themselves, automatically and without force. Your brain is pre-occupied by this man.

It's no good, Johnson. Better to give in. You're only prolonging it. Your fists are useless against handless arms, or against feet. The fight is unequal. You have fists to fight with. He has none. And this lack of his puts all the advantage on his side. For a blow with the fist is painful and damaging; on the right point it may be fatal. But a blow with a stump, while equally painful and damaging, is something more. You're realizing that. It stains honest combat with something anomalous. Its impact on the face is not only a blow: it is an innuendo. It makes you think when you ought to be fighting.

And with the blows from those handless arms there are the blows from what seems to be an open hand. They tear along your face and about your neck, and each blow brings nausea. Not because it's a blow from an open hand, but because you know that this man has no hands, and because the feel of it is too long for a hand. And then you know what it is. The man with no hands is fighting you with his feet. You could put up with that if he were using feet as men do use them; if he were kicking you. What sucks the strength from your knees is that his feet are behaving like hands. You feel as a dreamer feels when fighting the dead. You are already beaten, not by superior strength, but by blows from handless arms and from feet behaving as hands. And you know that it was your work that robbed him of his hands and left him to use his feet as hands.

And now you're down. And now one of those feet, more flexible and more full of life than any common hand, is on your neck. And the fog in this little derelict square deepens from brown to black. The foot presses and presses, very softly and very heavily; and your eyes become black fog and your mind becomes black fog. Black upon black, increasingly, until with the last rush of breath you are swallowed into a black void and a black silence and a black cessation of being.

And so, Johnson, you destroyed yourself, and because you

looked back you had the full bitterness of knowing that you destroyed yourself. For this blind and maimed and ferocious creature of the velvet steps was, of course, yourself. This creature without sight and without hands was your other self, your innermost guide, whom you so constantly thwarted and denied and broke. It was you who blinded him that he might not see your deeds, and it was the things you did with *your* hands which corrupted his, until he was left with none, and at last turned upon you. And then you looked back, and you saw yourself stalking yourself to destruction; and in the last blackness of terror you understood.

Happier for you if you had not looked back, and had not understood. For then, after a sojourn in the still dusk of Devachan, you would have returned to amend a wasted life by another pilgrimage. You would have returned blind and maimed to a life of struggle and frustration, poverty and contumely and pain. And you would have called it, with a shrug, what most men call it—Luck.

But you looked back. You are one of the few who die with full knowledge of their pursuer. So, with the blindness and mutilation, and the poverty and the pain, you will carry yet another tribulation. You will carry the tribulation of remembering *why* you are suffering.

TWO GENTLEMEN

This tale comes out of the lavender-blue distance of years and years ago, when street-bands were playing Sousa's new marches and when London had a Chinatown.

In that period, which to us is faintly aromatic, Young Fred was busy about the down-stream waterside earning his living. He did not earn his living by dealing in this or that commodity, or by manufacturing useful or useless things, or by working for other people's profit. He earned his living by the study of human nature. Novelists study human nature, and if they are good novelists they enrich the subject of their study. But almost every subject of Young Fred's study was a little poorer after Young Fred had studied him. As a gold-digger he could have given profitable lessons to the ladies of Broadway and the Riviera.

On the evening of a day that had been as dull as a wet day empty of business or friends can be, he sat in his back bedroom and stared at wet roofs and red chimney-pots. Things in his world were not going well. Money was running short; and worse—the supply of Mugs, the source of money, was also running short. He was faced with the problem of making bricks without clay, straw, old newspapers, or whatever bricks are made of. Black rain falling on grimy roofs is not a notable fount of inspiration, but Young Fred continued to stare through the window, and burn Woodbines, until he reached that state of semi-trance which is the only invitation the Muses recognize.

It was when he was well sunk in this mooning and all-forlorn state that the Muse came. It came not *via* the black rain but *via* a band which was playing—or would have said it was playing—at the corner of his street. It had just finished transmuting a Sousa march into a dirge, and was beginning an air from a new musical play called "The Geisha"—a song about "Ching-chang, China-man . . ." when the Muse descended and slipped an Idea into a corner of his mind. At the moment of its arrival it had no shape.

It was a mere homunculus of an idea. But within a few seconds it began to grow and to take an agreeable form. As it grew in his active mind, there emerged, from the corner where memory lives, two images which seemed fit companions for it. The images were Mr. Wo and Mr. Wum.

Young Fred had not made any close and deliberate study of Mr. Wo and Mr. Wum, but in his normal passings to and fro they had come under his unsleeping observation. He had noted them and their characteristics, and had filed them in his mental cabinet for possible future reference. They appeared to him now as the perfect vehicles for the materialization of the Idea.

They were close friends. Their friendship was not the casual, intimate, all-confessing friendship of common Englishmen. It was a friendship of dignities and reserves. A stranger, even if he could have eavesdropped on their private talk, would never have guessed they were deeply attached to each other. Neither knew much about the other, or sought to know; did not know even whether the other was rich or poor. Theirs was a philosophi-cal friendship. There was no warmth in their expressions; no Chinese equivalents of "Dear old chap" or "Man, you talk like a damfool." They went for slow walks together, talking little. They took meals at each other's homes, gravely and ceremonially; and though they had done this twice a week for some years, they still did it as though it were happening for the first time and they were the guest of a new acquaintance. When they did talk their speech was aloof and scrupulous in courtesy; mostly impersonal. But the bond between them, though imperceptible, was strong, and each knew that at any crisis he could call upon the other and be served.

Outside themselves, nobody knew, or had evidence for judging, that they were friends. Nobody, that is, save the excep-tionally gifted Young Fred; and you could no more hide things from him than you can from children at Christmas-time. It was in their peculiar friendship that he saw his opportunity, and the morning after the arrival of the Idea he set to work to put it into action.

His first visit was to a Post Office, where he bought a bill-stamp. On this bill-stamp he put some writing centring upon the figure of fifty pounds. He then went along the streets with that air of sober citizenship which is worn by all business-men when they are engaged upon some notably slimy bit of work. He maintained this air through most of that morning. At the suitable hour of eleven o'clock he called at the home of Mr. Wo, and desired a few minutes' private conversation.

In a little room at the back he explained to the courteous Mr. Wo that he was in business as a commercial and financial agent (which sounded as though it meant something, but gave no hint of its meaning) and that he had been approached, in the ordinary way of business, by Mr. Wum. Mr. Wum, it appeared, needed, until the end of the month, a small loan; a mere matter of fifty pounds. At this Mr. Wo exclaimed that of course he would readily lend his friend that sum, or two and three times that sum. To which Young Fred hastily interposed a quick No. No; that was not Mr. Wum's way. He had no desire to incommode his friends by introducing wretched commercial details between them. He preferred to keep business and friendship apart. That was why he had approached the obliging Young Fred. Young Fred, on his side, was wholly willing to make the advance, and had no doubts at all of Mr. Wum's personal integrity. Still, business was business and commercial risks were commercial risks. So, as he knew that Mr. Wo was a friend of Mr. Wum, it occurred to him that Mr. Wo would have no objection to guaranteeing the bill. Mr. Wo assured him that his surmise was sound, and that he would have pleasure in doing as requested. Whereupon Young Fred produced the bill, and Mr. Wo brought out his writing-brushes and endorsed it as blackly and solidly as ever a bill was endorsed.

Young Fred then thanked him, while assuring him, with true business courtesy, that it was, of course, a mere formality; and politely took his leave. The next two days he spent in unavoidable idleness, merely hanging about the streets to observe Mr. Wo and Mr. Wum on their walks, to note their demeanour to each other, and to let them see him. If his plan were miscarrying, Mr. Wo would surely challenge him during those two days. But though Mr. Wo distinctly saw him on three occasions, he made no sign; by which Young Fred guessed that he had calculated correctly.

On the third day he made another visit to the Post Office, and bought another bill-stamp, which also he covered with writing concerning the sum of fifty pounds. With this in his pocket he went gravely to the home of Mr. Wum, which was some distance from the home of Mr. Wo. To Mr. Wum he represented himself as a commercial and financial agent who had been approached, in the ordinary way of business, by Mr. Wo. Mr. Wo, it appeared, needed, until the end of the month, a small loan; a mere matter of fifty pounds. At this Mr. Wum exclaimed that, though it was somewhat inconvenient, and he was never well furnished with pounds, he would readily make every effort he could to provide his friend with that sum. To which Young Fred hastily interposed a quick No. No; that was not Mr. Wo's way. He had no desire to incommode his friends by introducing wretched commercial details between them. He preferred to keep friendship and business apart. That was why he had approached the obliging Fred. Fred, on his side, was wholly willing to make the advance, and had no doubts at all of Mr. Wo's personal integrity. Still, business was business, and . . . (see the foregoing).

When Young Fred left the shop he left it with the second bill-stamp blackly and solidly endorsed and backed by Mr. Wum.

For the next fifteen days he had nothing to do but wait for the end of the month. He spent the time in laying plans of another kind for some future business, and in observing Mr. Wo and Mr. Wum about the streets, and in letting them observe him. Neither made any sign of having seen him, save perhaps the faintest shade of embarrassment when he passed. To Mr. Wo his presence was a distressing reminder that his good friend Mr. Wum was in some difficulty, and was for the time being under an obligation to Mr. Wo for having backed his bill. To the sensitive Mr. Wo obligations on either side were pieces of grit whose existence a gentleman could not even mention. To Mr. Wum also the presence of Young Fred was a distressing reminder that his good friend Mr. Wo was in some difficulty, and was for the time being under an obligation to Mr. Wum for having backed his bill; and to the sensitive Mr. Wum obligations were what they were to Mr. Wo.

When, therefore, three days after the turn of the month, Young Fred called upon Mr. Wo and stated, with more than usual business gravity, that he regretted the necessity of his visit, he felt, not that it was a shame to take the money, but that he hadn't really earned it. It was too soft.

Mr. Wo heard with marked distress that his friend Mr. Wum had been so entangled by misfortune as to be unable to meet the bill. And when Young Fred explained that it was thus forced upon him (Young Fred), by ordinary commercial procedure, to ask Mr. Wo to honour his guarantee, Mr. Wo at once honoured it. In passing over the money, he set Young Fred's brain galloping by an assurance that he would willingly do as much again for his unfortunate friend.

At the home of Mr. Wum the report of Mr. Wo's default in the matter of the bill, owing to delay in expected remittances, caused similar and even stronger distress. To the distress caused by the thought of his friend's misfortune was added the distress of finding the fifty pounds.

But a visit to a compatriot, who was actually in business of the kind which Young Fred claimed as his, produced it. And Young Fred took a bus to the west, and spent the evening and a bit of the hundred pounds in the heavy English equivalent of Provençal song and sunburnt mirth.

*   *   *   *

The beautiful thing about the affair—apart from Young Fred's handling of it—is that while many a friendship has been wrecked by the backing of a bill, this friendship was thereby strengthened. Each was so gratified at having been, as he thought, of service to his friend, that he soon forgot the gritty fact that his friend was under an obligation to him; and they became still more drawn to each other.

Such delicacy between friends has its merits. It enriches the texture of the friendship itself, and it enables the Young Freds of this world to live in comfort. Still, so far as the pocket is concerned, the moral is that friends should be as open and blunt about mutual service as City men are. Between whom, as you know, the Young Freds get no chance.

THE BLACK COURTYARD

Nobody saw him. In the late evening of that winter day he came creeping from that riverside courtyard—a courtyard thick with darkness, and alive only with silence and the eyes of blind houses; and nobody saw him. He was slim, and his body in movement was elastic. He walked with a rhythmic padding step. He presented himself to the eye as a heavy overcoat, a soft hat, and a muffler.

That evening, in all parts of London, was an evening of intense darkness; starless and heavy with rain. But in the east the already dark streets were put to confusion by a river-mist. In this mist the lamps were dabs of phosphorescence. The shop-lights blessed only a foot of the pavement, and even the torches of the stalls could achieve no more than a luminosity which was no light at all.

Belated shoppers moved in and out of the little shops in the form of floating faces. The narrow thoroughfare was populous with the creatures of all nations, but amid the shifting veils of mist one could not know white man from Cingalese, nor yellow man from negro, nor honest man from skulker. They were no more than spectral shapes of Man.

Perrace, the muffled figure coming from the courtyard, was one of them.

Nowhere was the darkness more intense than there. So intense was it that it seemed to have a quality of life. It menaced the eyes and pressed upon the face. Its silence seemed to whisper upon the ears. It was an organism of blackness whose tendrils almost throttled the breath. But to Perrace and his purposes this profusion of darkness was kind.

As he came from the courtyard the river sent to land the howl of a foghorn, and from distant byways came the cries of roysterers. A banjo could be heard; a gramophone; an over-tuned radio. Thick, rough life, and the rumour of unseen life, surged all about him; but Perrace, padding his solitary way, was concerned with death.

He padded along the High Street. He padded up Love Lane. He padded along Cable Street and along Brook Street, and as he passed from one street to another the tempo of his padding increased, and gave him the air of one in flight.

He *was* in flight. He was fleeing not from fear of arrest, but from fear of a courtyard thick with darkness, deaf to noise, and alive only with the eyes of blind houses. Those houses had seen nothing; in that darkness they could not, even unshuttered, have seen; yet their very blindness had shot him with a deeper fear than the fear of capture. They and the courtyard in which they stood were before him now. They were like figures threatening. They seemed to say "We didn't see, but we *know*. And we're going to make you pay." In the effort to shake them from his eyes he padded faster and faster. He turned into Stepney Causeway, and loped along it, and did not fall to his customary rhythm until he came out to the misty glitter and clamour of Commercial Road.

There he paused, uncertain of his next action. But his mind told him that action was imperative: he must not linger; he must not be seen here. He debated by which way he should return home, but so many ways came to his mind that he could not decide upon one for thought of the others. Then, when he had hesitated some two minutes, a string of westward buses, lumbering out of the mist, settled the matter for him. Their presence brought him out of his paralysis; with automatic movements he boarded the first of them and climbed to the top. He sat down with a heavy sigh.

Life on a sudden seemed unaccountably strange. He was still alive, breathing through his nose, seeing with his eyes. Yet his state of being was not the state of being of a few hours ago. He was sitting on a bus; a bus like other buses; but charged to his mind with some intense and un-bus-like essence. Like that courtyard and that darkness and those houses, it seemed alive. This was Perrace sitting on the bus—Perrace, himself yet not himself. The same hair, the same eyes, the same hands, the same flow of conscious memory. Yet a Perrace who was a stranger to him.

At the bottom of his mind was a faint feeling, or perhaps a faint hope, that soon he would wake up and find himself warm and comfortable in his bed at Kingsland Road. The top of his mind knew that he wouldn't.

He looked down at his overcoat. It was his overcoat, his quite ordinary overcoat. Since the day he bought it he had never really seen it. Now he saw it, and the coat, too, seemed to come to life. He had put it on that afternoon as casually as he always put it on. But that was before the Idea had come to him. He knew that he would not take it off casually. It was now an experienced over-coat; a dramatic overcoat; it had been in that courtyard. It might even become a famous overcoat.

At that thought he shivered, and felt sick. Events of the last two hours recurred to him. They had the complexion of that truth which is insistently truth but incomprehensible by human reason. That accursed courtyard had created them.

He recalled the courtyard, and he recalled the dark room, and he recalled the bent, questioning figure of the old man. And he recalled the old man lying still and pulseless on the floor. And he recalled the escape by the window. He recalled how often he had haunted that courtyard, and how often the courtyard had haunted *him*. He recalled how it had set things in his mind. How it had lived there, peacefully malignant, suggesting sin, but never the price of sin. How it had beckoned him to give it the story for which it was made. He recalled the many times when he had looked into it and looked at a certain house, and had thought of the hundreds of notes which the stupid feeble old man was known to hoard; notes which meant so much to one who was out of a job. He recalled how he had planned the affair over drinks in the—what was the name of the place? He recalled how he had first brushed the idea aside—its mere presence had given him a fit of tremors—and how, later, he had gibed at himself for a coward, and screwed himself up to it. He recalled how clear it had been in his mind during the long evening.

It was when he had come to set it to action that it had gone blurred and feverish. Coming out of the courtyard had been like a waking-up. He could not recall entering the house; he could only dimly recall being there. He could not recall what he had started to do; he could recall only what had been done. He could not recall what desk or cupboard or safe he had opened. He could not even recall the contents of the room. He could recall only its darkness and its shape. He could not recall finding the money, nor, if he found it, what he had done with it. He knew only that he had brought none of it away. He could not recall the entrance of the miser to the room; he could recall only the patch on the dark floor.

The two really vivid memories were of going into the courtyard, and of coming out of it. Once or twice he had a feeling that it had never happened, but in the moment of the feeling a dim glow of memory told him that the feeling was merely a reflection of his agonized wish. He was suffering and making forlorn efforts to escape the suffering.

Above the imps of thought that were dancing on his brain hovered the word *MURDER*. It seemed ludicrous, insane almost, that this word could be fastened to the name Perrace. This Perrace was known to his few acquaintances as a fellow like other fellows. A fellow who had no life beyond the life which society allows to a poor man—the life of a steady worker, a respectable nine-o'clock-to-six-o'clock employee who held no opinions to attract remark, who did nothing to-day that would be remembered to-morrow, and to whom nothing outside routine ever happened. And now he had broken the bounds of routine and opened its quiet to the claws of peril and dread.

Never again would he sleep securely. Never again would he walk the streets carelessly. Life and death had broken in upon his coma, and he, who had hitherto faced only the shadow of them, must now, through the memory of a black courtyard, face the reality. And he was not ready to face it. He had acted before he had reached the mood for action. He was unprepared. He hadn't *meant* to do it. Yet they would brand him, and if they seized him they would talk about him as though he were an animal, and not Perrace, the ordinary, likeable fellow. And then they would kill him.

He had always been assured, as most of us are, that while other men might commit murder, he, Perrace, never could. He had read in newspapers of men who committed murder, but he had read of them as monsters, remote creatures of another plane and another state; not as fellow-creatures of the world he lived in. They were not men who rode in buses and worked in offices and were sometimes out of a job, and sat in tea-shops and went to whist-drives and did a bit of gardening on Saturday afternoons. They were Murderers; something apart.

Yet this night he had been presented in that courtyard with himself in that shape, a self which he knew was his but which he could not recognize; a self from which he revolted. Perrace, the ordinary likeable fellow, turned within an hour into a creature who belonged in that affrighting gallery in the basement of Tussaud's.

It was ludicrous. It was like a tale of a millionaire forging a cheque for five pounds. But a persistent spot in his brain said: "Yes —but true." His quiescent mind said: "It isn't. It isn't. I didn't do it. I didn't." His active mind drowned it with "You did. You did. You may not have meant to, but you did."

Under these conflicting mental revolutions he suffered a loathing of his existence, and a bilious horror of the black courtyard. It was beginning to torment him. It danced in his mind, and his mind interpreted it to his sight and his body as clammy shadows touching the skin. In that long ride through Stepney, Aldgate and the City, he saw, wherever he looked, a courtyard thick with darkness, deaf to noise and alive only with the eyes of blind houses. A courtyard that might tempt a man and encourage him to all manner of enormities, and then turn upon him.

He left the bus at the Bank and caught a last bus for Shoreditch. He was aware that he moved rationally and spoke rationally, but this behaviour, he knew, came from the last automatic movements of his real self. That self, the self he had known these thirty years, was now lying numb and bemused. It seemed to be fading from him, his being was slowly passing into possession of a new stranger-self. He did not like this new self, and fought against surrendering to it. But there was no question of his surrendering. It was insistently taking possession of him—a nervous, feverish self that had crept out of a courtyard thick with darkness and deaf to noise. He wondered whether all murderers were possessed like this. From their behaviour in court he felt that they were not.

Murder seemed to make them stronger instead of weaker, more callous instead of more sensitive.

In his room at Kingsland Road he took off his overcoat and hung it on a coat-hanger. From the other side of the room he turned to look at it. It seemed to look back at him. He took off his boots and looked at them, and they too seemed different from other boots. Mighty and terrible boots. At any moment, he foolishly felt, coat and boots might become articulate. The sight of them began to fret his already fretted mind. He gathered them up and stowed them into a cupboard. For the next half-hour he padded about the room. From time to time he brushed his arm across his eyes. Somewhere on his retina was the image of a black courtyard. He went to the mirror to see if he could find it. Then realized his own folly, and gave a weak laugh, and again felt sick.

Under this sickness he crept to the bed and fell on it, and, not expecting sleep, slept. But in the sleep he was aware that he was sleeping on the stones of a black courtyard.

He awoke as Perrace, to a few shreds of his own self not yet destroyed; but in a few seconds, when fully awake, he realized that he was no longer Perrace. He was a creature out of a black courtyard, and he existed only in relation to that courtyard. He was its prisoner. Over-riding the memory of last night's affair was the more awful presence of this manifestation. He was in the world, but he was enclosed from it. He could see it only through the shadows of his courtyard.

He strove to shoulder it away by movement. He got up and exercised himself. He plunged his head and neck into cold water. He went over himself with a rough towel. He felt too sick to eat the breakfast his landlady had prepared, but he drank two cups of tea and nibbled some bread. At ten o'clock he went out and walked wherever the streets led him.

Throughout the day he loafed about the main streets of the poorer quarters. He wandered from Oxford Street to St. John's Wood, from there to Camden Town, then to Finsbury Park, to Highgate, to Islington, to Euston Road, to Charing Cross, Waterloo Road, to Kennington, Camberwell, Peckham.

After some hours of walking at his gentle padding pace, his mind cleared and things began to adjust themselves. In the light he regained something of his old self; a little of the everyday confidence he had known before yesterday. He began to feel that he had exaggerated the affair and his own fears. In the afternoon sun the black courtyard seemed far away in distance and in time and in conception. Neither the morning papers nor the evening papers carried a line about that courtyard. No doubt in a day or two it would fade from his mind as other incidents faded from the mind. Within a month he would perhaps have to make an effort to recall anything about that courtyard. It might be weeks yet before the secret was discovered, and there would be nothing by which they could connect it with him. In a momentary facetiousness the thought occurred to him that anyway it was his first offence.

But when night came upon the city he learned that the courtyard was only beginning its work upon him. He had not noted the approach of dusk, and he was walking along Rye Lane, Peckham, when the horror descended. The haunting took material shape.

He was certain that it was Rye Lane. He had seen its name on a plate at a corner. Yet, turning suddenly from a brilliant shopwindow, he found that he was not in Rye Lane. Shops and lights had disappeared. He was in that black courtyard.

He could feel its darkness upon his face; he could hear its crowding silence; he could see the sightless eyes of its houses. A dry choking seized his throat. He turned in panic to get out of the place. He tore through the courtyard, and down the entrance alley. As he ran, he was aware of shouts and noises. Dimly he saw scared faces about him, and heard the grinding of brakes. He had a vision of a lorry striking his shoulder, of a bus-driver making a scowling face. But they were phantasmagoria floating across the fact of the black courtyard, and he gave them no attention. Every nerve of him was centred on getting out of the courtyard.

But he was not to get out of it. He was its prisoner. He thought he had got out of it, but, on crossing the road and taking the first turning, he found he was in it again. There it was, in Peckham, clear to the eye—a riverside courtyard thick with darkness. This time he fought his way out of it, and stood at its entrance gasping. Real people moving along Rye Lane passed him as shadows, and an elfin voice came out of the air—"How's a chap get like that so early in the evening? Quick work eh?"

The words, faint as an echo in a valley, suggested something to him, though for some time he could not locate the suggestion. Then it came to him in clear terms—a drink. A drink was what he wanted. He hadn't had any drink or any food all day. A drink might rid him of this horror. But the idea of a drink brought a crowded, noisy bar; and he could not face a crowded, noisy bar. He wondered whether he might find a quiet, side-street place near by.

A little bland-faced man was passing the mouth of the alley. He stopped him. "Er—could you tell me if there's a quiet little bar anywhere near here? Little place a respectable man can go to?" The bland-faced man looked at him. "Yes. But a respectable man can go anywhere, can't he? Still, if you want a quiet place, go up here and take the first on the left."

He thanked the bland-faced man, and went swiftly up the half-lit road. Projecting from the corner of the first turning on the left he saw a signboard—*The Anchor and Hope.* He saw it as a portent. Reaching the first turning, he went to the left, anticipating the soothing effect of the drink. He went to the left, and walked into a courtyard thick with darkness and deaf to noise.

He came out of it cursing the bland-faced man, and sobbing. He fell into a loping run. He pressed his fingers to his eyes, and rubbed his face. He uttered automatic noises. His voice said "Damn—damn—damn," and many coarser words.

In a long blue-lit street his breathing made him pause. Looking about him, he saw that the street was a street and its lamps were lamps. He took off his hat and rubbed his hands round his head. Nerves, he told himself. Nerves; just nerves. That's what it was. That courtyard wasn't there. Couldn't be there. An attack of nerves. He was just *seeing* it. Well, he wouldn't see it. It wasn't there at all. It was just nerves. Nerves. Nerves.

But with that discovery he learned that he had admitted another enemy. He had admitted a word, and the word, once admitted, pattered on his brain until even the haunting of the courtyard seemed less horrible. It walked with his feet, and beat with his pulse, and floated before his eyes. Nerves. . . . Nerves. . . .

Nerves. . . . Nerves. The shape of the word, as it spelt its letters before him, was of something spidery and ghastly. The sound of it became like a wail from an asylum. Nerves. . . . Nerves. . . . Nerves. . . . Or like the last rush of breath from a dying old man. Nerves. . . . Nerves. . . . Nerves. . . . Eugh. . . . Eugh. . . . Eugh.

"You better go home," he told himself. "You better go home. That's the best place."

He went home. Somehow he found his way back to Kingsland Road. He went by buses that glided through one black courtyard after another, and he walked through black courtyards. In a shop in one of these courtyards he bought a quart bottle of stout, and at last he came to his room in a black courtyard, and the room itself was a black courtyard.

He sat on the bed in that courtyard and said "Oh. . . . Oh. . . ." and "Oh, dear. . . . Oh, dear. . . ." He poured a glass of the stout, and drank it off. It soothed him, and within a few minutes the room began to resume the features of his old room. He drank another glass, and sat with hands limply hanging over knees. "I must be going mad. I must be going mad. Oh, if only . . ." He drank another glass; and soon the stout, working upon the exhaustion of the day's walk, brought sleepiness. It brought, too, the complete removal of the courtyard. As he sat on the bed, it faded from eye and mind, and all that he could see resolved itself into his own familiar room.

But in sleep it came back. It came back in all its detail. The courtyard itself, the shuttered house, the dark room, the bent old man. They danced and whirled about his consciousness. They were figures. They were colours. They were sounds and smells. They changed their form; they changed their character; they shifted from solid to vapour. But always, whatever their form or figuration, in their impact upon the brain they were black courtyard, shuttered house, dark room, bent old man. It seemed that he had not finished with them. It seemed that they were beckoning him. At times their attitude penetrated to his consciousness as friendly and encouraging. It seemed that there was something they wanted of him. But when he awoke, he awoke with a moan and a gasp and a sensation of choking.

The day repeated the yesterday. In the thin winter sunlight

he was safe, but once the night had come the courtyard fastened upon him and enclosed him. London was one black courtyard. Beyond it he could see gleaming tram-cars and buses, and blazing shops, and streets crowded with faces dull or bright. But he could reach none of them. He could not get out. He could only pad round and round his courtyard, moaning.

Late in the evening, an idea came to him. "See a doctor." Somewhere in the everlasting black courtyard, a few paces back, he had noted a brass plate. With some trouble he found it again, and fifteen minutes later he was sitting in a pleasant consulting-room. The atmosphere of the room, the furniture, the bright fire, the dog's-eared back-numbers of illustrated papers, restored him to a sense of everyday. Here were peace and warmth; nothing foolish, it seemed, could live here. It was a haven of sanity and sense to which the sailing courtyard could not penetrate.

By the time the doctor came in he was collected and calm. He gave a fictitious name and address as easily as though it were his own, and began to state his case.

"Know anything about nerves, doctor?"

"A good deal of the little we can know. What's the trouble?"

"Haunted."

"Mmmmm. I see. Being followed, eh?"

"Oh, no. No. Not that. But . . . wherever I go I see a dark courtyard. A dark courtyard. It seems to close me in, like. Even Regent Street becomes a dark courtyard. Black."

"Yes. Well, there's lots of dark courtyards in London. You *would* see a lot if you go about much. There's one or two off Regent Street."

"Yes, but. . . . It's everywhere. Even at home. Though I feel all right here. This is the first place I've been free of it for two days. It don't seem able to get at me here. Perhaps it can't come where there's strong people. I was wondering if you could give me some——" His voice broke. His eyes were staring past the doctor. "Oh, God—look—it's there. It's there!"

He was half-way from his chair, his hand pointing to something behind the doctor. "The window. I can see it outside the window." The doctor did not look towards the window. He kept his eyes on his patient. "What is it you're seeing?" "It's there—

outside the window—the black courtyard. All dark. And little houses."

"Yes, yes. Of course. I know."

"What d'you mean—yes, yes? Look yourself. Look through that window. Tell me what's really there."

"A dark courtyard. With little houses."

"You—you—— You playing with me? Humouring me? Or——"

"Of course not, man. If I look out of that window I can see a dark courtyard with little houses. Same as you can. And everybody else. I've been seeing it every night since I've been here —these twelve years."

"It's there, then?"

"Of course it's there.... Now then—sit down. Take it easy. Let's try the old reflexes."

There was a ten-minute examination. The doctor went to his desk and made some notes. He turned to the patient. "What you want is a change. Complete change and rest. You're just on the edge of a breakdown. But before you can get anything out of change and rest you must get this thing off your mind. You've got a dark courtyard on your mind. Something unpleasant must have happened to you in a dark courtyard. Well, the right thing to do is to go back to that courtyard, and——"

"Go *back!*"

"Yes. Don't look so scared, man. It's the cleanest way. Go back to that identical courtyard and those little houses. At night. And face whatever it's got. Go over it all again in the identical spot. Challenge it."

"You don't know what you're asking."

"Yes I do. I'm asking you to make a drastic effort. It's the only way. Nerves are like mad dogs. Run away, and they'll get you. Face 'em, and you're all right. You must go back to that place. At night, mind you. Face it out. And if you face it and go over whatever happened there, you'll probably find that the second experience will cancel the effect of the first. A mental medicine."

"I don't think I could. You don't understand. You wouldn't—"

"You can do it. If you make yourself. Anyway, try to. Get as far as you can. I can suggest nothing else. *I* can't rid you of this thing.

Only yourself can do that. Nervous troubles can only be cured by the patient. The doctor can't cure 'em."

*   *   *   *

For five nights more he lived with his horror. Through the orchestration of his waking and sleeping life it recurred and persisted like a main theme gone wild. Life, once an affair of light beat and homely tune, had become a fugue upon a black courtyard. And it seemed that there was no stopping it. Nothing he could do would obliterate it. Memory operated upon nothing else. It carried it and dandled it and frisked it under his very eyes, until his surface and his core were a black courtyard at midnight.

It was not until his whole being had become a scream of "What can I do? What can I do?" that he saw the only thing to do. A perilous thing, certainly, but a thing that would lead at least to escape from *this*. He felt that he could live no longer with it. If, then, death was the only escape, he must take that way. But not by the river or the gas-fire. Those ways were certain and fixed. The doctor's way was almost equally certain of ending in disaster, but it was the "almost" that decided him to take it.

If the police were waiting for him; expecting him, as a bungling amateur, to follow the false popular tradition and return to the place—well, that way of ending, hideous as it was, could be no worse than this present horror. And it was possible . . . it might be that they were not waiting for him. He had searched each day the morning and evening papers, but never a line had he seen about any discovery in any riverside court. It might be that nothing had become known. It might be that the doctor's advice was not only sound but safe; that this one secret visit would indeed ease him of his burden. And that he might not only lose burden and danger of the law's penalty, but win the money he had forgotten to bring away. Suppose he risked it?

With that, resolution came to him. His spirits rose. His nerves ceased their jangling. He would risk it, and he would go that night. It seemed a propitious night—the exact week from *the* night—and it would at least mean action and a result of some sort.

So at ten o'clock that night he went. In Kingsland Road the air was clear, but by the river there was again a mist, and again he passed through its streets as no more than a heavy overcoat, a soft hat, and a muffler. He found himself strangely careless of what might be waiting for him, and he walked with his usual padding step. He felt in good health—confident and strong; and when he came to the little street from which the alley led, he went lightly along it. He turned swiftly into the alley, and thence came once more into a courtyard thick with darkness, deaf to noise, and alive only with the eyes of blind houses.

For some seconds he stood still. But he saw nothing to alarm him, and heard nothing, and with quick, quiet steps he moved to the house in the corner.

There he waited. He looked round the court—challenged it, dared it. It made no demonstration. It did not threaten him. It did not frighten him. It was a court only, like other courts. Now that he was there, it seemed well disposed towards him. He wondered how he could have been so foolish as to let it weigh upon him. He must have been out of sorts last week.

He turned again to the little house. Yes; this was where he had stood, just at this shutter, just above this grating that made a right-angle with the basement window. He bent to the grating and listened. No clear sound at all came to him—only a whispering wave of silence. He touched the grating, and found it as loose as he had left it last week. It would lift easily. He lifted it, and as he lifted it a shaft of memory lit his mind.

He stood with it in his hand, and remembered that this was exactly how he had stood a week ago when he had come over faint. Exactly—the same attitude, the same finger of the left hand supporting the grating, the same movement of the right arm towards the window, the same——

And then he found himself in action. He had not directed himself to this action, but he *was* in action. He was underneath the grating, crouching in the tiny aperture before the window. His knife was working on the catch of the window. The catch slid back. With delicate fingers he lowered the window, and within four seconds he was in the house.

He switched on his torch, and its darting light showed him a dirty unkempt kitchen. But here the shaft of memory blurred

and faded. He could not recall this kitchen. He moved the torch
and it showed him a door and a staircase. He could not recall that
staircase; but even while trying to recall it he found himself as-
cending it with his rhythmic padding. He reached the top and saw
a passage leading to the front door, and in the passage two other
doors, and another staircase. This again was strange to him, but
he found himself on those stairs, going softly up, and he found
himself in another and tinier passage, also with two doors. He
found himself trying the handle of one of them, and working
upon its lock with a wire key. And then he found the door open
and himself in the room.

He darted his torch about the room and saw a chest, and
a bureau, and a copper box. He went first to the chest, worked
upon its lock, and routed among its contents. He was blank of
all thought and all feeling; blank of all memory of repeating last
week; blank of all concern of the dead old man. He was just an
organism of action. At the bottom of the chest his hand touched
a packet that rustled. He brought it out, and his torch showed
him what it was. He thrust it into his pocket, and dived again, and
found another and another. Pound-notes in packets.

The chest yielded three more packets. When he felt that he
had exhausted it, he turned to the bureau. A few twists of his wire
key opened it, and he dived his hand into its drawers. His hand
found more and more, and he filled his pockets with them.

It was just when he was turning from the bureau to the copper
box that he heard a sound. Scarcely a noise; just that faint disturbance of the air which is made by the presence of a living
creature. He turned his torch flat to the floor, and with an un-
directed movement reached to the fire-place. His hand found a
fire-iron. As his fingers closed upon it, he moved swiftly and shot
the beam of the torch at arm's length towards the door.

It showed, just inside the door, the bent figure of an old man.

At that sight he knew what he had to do. Something that he
had not been ready to do before, but for which he was now ready.

The old man made a faint cluck and shuffled three paces
towards him. Perrace took one pace, and met him. From behind
his back the fire-iron came down on the bent head—one, two—
the old man fell—three, four.

He dropped the fire-iron and stepped back. His breath came out in a long rush, and with it came all the weight of fear that had been his burden. In that moment some immaterial shuttles seemed to readjust themselves, and bring into being a Perrace that was himself, but stronger. He was conscious of elation. No courtyard now could hold any terrors for him. He had rounded upon his haunting and materialized it. The live idea he had killed, as he had killed the old man. It was now a dead fact.

He shot the light of the torch upon the old man to satisfy himself that the thing was fully done; then switched off the torch, buttoned his coat, and gently felt his way down the stairs.

He came out from the basement window into a courtyard thick with darkness, and alive only with silence and the eyes of blind houses. This time it said nothing to him. He scarcely noticed it. It was just a place where he had cleared up something that had puzzled him. He padded from it into the alley, and so into the misted side-streets, and melted into other narrow streets until he appeared in firm shape at Fenchurch Street station. There, mixing with the crowd coming from a late Tilbury train, he took a taxi to Soho, and from Soho another taxi to Euston. From Euston he took a bus to Dalston, and from there he walked home.

In his room he made a close examination of his clothes, and found that he had been lucky. He stowed his money away in a suitcase and two boxes, and softly whistled a little tune. He went to bed, and slept better than he had slept for many weeks.

He slept until ten o'clock, when his landlady woke him to tell him that two important-looking men wanted to see him.

THE GRACIOUS GHOSTS

There are some houses, grim, reticent houses, which should have a ghost and haven't. There are others, bright, airy, happy houses, which shouldn't have a ghost but have one. The bright little house overlooking Regent's Park, which Lyssom had just taken, was one of these. It had an overdose; it had two ghosts.

They were not disturbing ghosts, save in the sense that all ghosts are disturbing. There was nothing eerie about them. They made no effort to "get at" people. They did not cause doors to open, or knock china about, or make rustlings at midnight. They were, indeed, remarkably well-behaved, and as nice-looking a pair of ghosts as one could wish to have about the place. They were almost company for Lyssom, and, after the first shock of the realization that they *were* ghosts, he found himself accepting them without even a raised eyebrow. He was a lonely, middle-aged fellow, stout and bald, and it was pleasant for him to have something bright and young to look at.

For these ghosts were boy and girl. They were not Elizabethan, nor even Victorian. The girl was about seventeen and the boy about twenty; and, judged by their style of dress, they belonged to the immediate post-war period—about 1919. They first appeared while Lyssom was at dinner a few evenings after he had moved in. It was September, and still daylight. He was reaching for the bottle of Moselle when his hand stopped and his eyes remained fixed on the French window which opened to his little garden. Mentally he said, "What the devil——" then opened his mouth to say, "I beg your pardon, but——" Then he closed his mouth and said nothing, for he realized that the pleasant young couple who had thus suddenly appeared in his dining-room weren't really there.

They were there to sight, clear enough, but they were standing against the frame of the French window, and just as he was about to speak he noted that though their bodies were directly against the frame he could still see the frame through the young man's shirt-front. He sat motionless, watching. Then he smiled. The boy and girl looked at each other; then looked away; then looked again at each other. Then the girl's hand moved about an inch towards the boy's. And the boy's hand moved and clasped it, and lifted it and kissed it. Next moment Lyssom was looking at a French window, and nothing else.

In the fortnight that followed he got the habit of waiting for his visitors to appear. Their presences appeared only three times a day. At breakfast-time in the hall, looking at each other with morning smiles; around dinner-time by the French window; and between eleven and midnight at the foot of the stairs—the girl halfway upstairs, the boy at the foot. For Lyssom it was rather like a story; he developed an interest in the young shadows and wanted to know what happened to them, and why.

He wondered why they always appeared in the same places, and why the thing stopped at smiles and that impulsive hand-kissing. He wondered whether a motor-smash, a sudden illness, or a fire had claimed both of them. Sometimes there were breaks in their appearance—three or four days when there was no sign of them; and then they would appear regularly again, three times a day. This gave him further matter for speculation, and as his time was his own he did a good deal of speculating on the problem. But he could devise no explanation that satisfied him. He could only live with these amiable shadows, and wonder.

Then one afternoon he spoke of the affair to an acquaintance at the club, a man with a taste for oddities. The acquaintance, after listening some time with merely polite attention, became alert and showed a more serious attention. He woke up when Lyssom was describing the young people, their faces and hair and dress. "Oh, really. . . . Ah. . . . 'M. . . . Interesting that. Let me see, where is this new place of yours?" Lyssom gave him the address. "Ah, yes; of course. I ought to have remembered. Yes—the Panberrys' old place. I know it. Been empty some years, hasn't it? Care to ask me to dinner one evening?"

"Why, yes, if you don't mind a bachelor dinner?"

"Don't mind? Bachelors' dinners are always the best, old man. They have time for dining. Dinner is an event with them, not a quick prelude to the drawing-room. What evening?"

Lyssom named an evening. "But I don't know whether you'll see them, if that's your idea. Maybe it's only me that can see them."

"I'll chance that. I'm fairly sensitive to things of that sort if they're about. And I know that house quite well, so I won't be an intruder or an alien influence."

On an evening of the next week Lyssom and the acquaintance, Carton, were at the dining-table in the Regent's Park house waiting for the soup. It was a round table, and Lyssom had placed his guest and himself so that both had a clear view of the window and the garden. Lyssom's man had just served the soup, and retired, when Lyssom looked quickly at Carton to see if he were "receiving" anything. He was. His hand holding his spoon was arrested in mid-air, and Lyssom saw that he was seeing just what he himself was seeing. He was staring at the French window, but he seemed rather more surprised than Lyssom had expected him to be. His face, indeed, registered blank astonishment. He had spoken as though he had seen ghosts before, yet now he was staring at the window with wide eyes and a puzzled mouth. Explosively he said "But——" and went on staring. For quite a minute he stared without moving—"struck silly," as Lyssom expressed it.

Then, at the moment when the hands of the young figures met each other, he set down his spoon. Still keeping his eyes on the window he lost his vacant look, and his face broke into an amused smile. Twice he nodded his head, as though something had been made clear to him; and in a little murmur he said, "I see.... I see." Then he turned to Lyssom. "If you want those ghosts laid I think I can lay them."

"I don't know. They don't disturb me. I find them rather company. Of course, they might upset some of my guests some time. People get so scared of the unusual. But how would you go about it?"

"Oh, there won't be any fuss. No chalk circles or pentacles or candles. Quite a simple matter. And I think it'd be better to lay them. For their own sake. It's a duty which the haunted owe to the haunters."

"But they don't look miserable. All the ghosts I've heard or read about are unhappy. Something on their minds, and they died before they settled it, and can't rest until it's settled. But these don't look like that. They look quite happy."

"None the less, they'll be happier when they're laid; and I think I can do it. They're a nice couple, and they deserve it."

"*Were* a nice couple, you mean."

"Yes, of course. *Were.* I forgot. They look so alive."

"When do you think you'd like to try the laying?"

"Oh, one night next week. I'll telephone you. I may need some help. There's a man who knows a lot more about these things than I do, and he could probably advise me. I'll let you know."

Late the next week Lyssom had a telephone call from Carton. Carton had got in touch with his friend, and wanted to bring him along to dinner. "Nice chap. Research chemist. And there's a woman I know I'd like to bring, too. Charming woman. You'll like her. Scots, and has something of the Scots' second-sight. So she might be useful in a case like this. She's coming down from Scotland to-morrow for a few days; so shall we say Wednesday?"

Lyssom said Wednesday; and that evening Carton arrived with his two friends, Philip Rode and Miss Maclaren. They were, as he had said, pleasant people, and they seemed immediately at home with their host and his place. Each of them had the slim face and grey eyes of the spiritual type, and Lyssom was aware of a strong, warm feeling in the room which suggested that things were about to happen. The preparatory atmosphere, he thought, for the ghost-laying. The dinner went agreeably, and they talked of this and that, but nothing was said about ghosts. Miss Maclaren appeared to be much interested in research chemistry, and asked many questions which the chemist expounded as fully as he could. Carton talked of recent doings in Whitehall, and the chemist, when he wasn't answering questions, listened to his host's talk of the latest French painters.

After dinner Lyssom showed his collection of modern French works, and when that was done, and it came to whisky-and-soda time, he began to look at Carton, wondering when he would start the business they had gathered for. But Carton was deep in the subject of Japanese expansion, and kept in it until 11 o'clock, when Miss Maclaren said she must go. The chemist asked if he might drive her home—he had his little two-seater outside—and could he drop Carton somewhere? Carton said he was staying awhile; he wanted to convert Lyssom on the question of sea and air power; and the two guests went off alone. Their phrase of thanks to Lyssom seemed genuine.

It was not until they had gone that Lyssom remembered something. "Rather odd, Carton—they've appeared every evening for the last fortnight, but to-night, when we wanted 'em, they didn't appear. I forgot about it at dinner. Forgot to look for 'em. Was it hostile presences, d'you think? Though those young people seemed quite the sympathetic sort."

"No; it wasn't that."

"'M. Well, did your friends give you any advice how to handle it? And when are you going to make a start?"

"No. I didn't ask 'em. No need."

"Really? You know how to manage it, then?"

"No. No need for it now. It's done."

"Done? When was it done?"

"Early this evening. Before we arrived. You won't see your young ghosts any more."

"How was it done?"

"Well, you noticed they didn't appear this evening at the French window. They couldn't. They were at the table."

"What—behind us?"

"No, with us."

"I didn't see 'em."

"You did. Philip Rode and Miss Maclaren. They were your ghosts. I was expecting you'd recognize 'em, though they are both fifteen years older than their ghosts."

"Rode and Miss Maclaren? Ghosts? But they're alive. Ghosts are of dead people."

"Not necessarily. Ghosts of living people can haunt a beloved spot as effectively as ghosts of the dead—if they're a strong spiritual type and if they have reason for thinking and thinking about a certain place. That's what was happening here. Those two spent a summer here when he was about twenty, with the Panberrys. I was a guest part of the time, and watched the start of their affair.

Then there was a break of some sort; quarrel, perhaps. I don't know. But they lost sight of each other. You can see, though, what happened later. Always they were thinking of each other and projecting themselves, in memory, to this place where they spent those rapturous hours of first love. But with such unusual force that they became visible. I recognized 'em at once as soon as their ghosts appeared at the French window the other evening. And I knew they were both still living. So I laid your ghost by asking 'em separately to meet me in town, saying I'd like to see 'em again. Then, when I'd brought 'em together early this evening, I dragged 'em along to the place where their affair began. And they laid their ghosts by their physical presence."

JACK WAPPING

At half-past four of a January morning, young Jack Wapping was recalled from an unconsciousness free of dreams into a consciousness full of that morning and the prospect of the Daily Sweat. The thing that recalled him was a peremptory carillon played upon his half-crown alarm clock. This carillon was being played at the same time upon alarm clocks in a hundred curtained bedrooms of Spadgett Street. It was Industry's call to arms, and Jack Wapping obeyed it with as much concern as the soldier obeys *réveillé*; and for a stronger reason. The soldier's failure carries loss of liberty and increased servitude. Jack Wapping's failure would have meant freedom from servitude and increased liberty—liberty to walk the streets and to owe for his rent, and to seek State relief for himself and his young wife.

He obeyed it as he obeyed it upon three hundred mornings of the year; first by giving it an unspoken imprecation (he was not sufficiently awake to swear aloud); then by sitting up in bed and rubbing his head. His next movements were to reach out and switch off its icy tinkle; to fumble for matches and light a candle; to get out of bed and stretch and shiver; and to huddle on the elements of dress.

Half-clothed in vest and trousers, he took the candle and, with delicate blundering, so as not to wake young Mrs. Wapping, he left his two-room home (with use of kitchen) and descended to that kitchen. There he set a kettle on the gas-stove; then turned to the sink and put head and neck under the tap and got busy with strong-smelling soap. He did no Daily Dozen or Half-dozen. He had neither the time for them nor the need of them. His daily tasks gave him sufficient physical exercise to set up several sedentary workers. With a soft whistling of the theme song of the last talkie he had seen he dried himself on a rough roller towel. He did not shave; for him that point of toilet belonged to the evening when he returned from work and was his own man. But at a six-inch mirror he brushed and combed his hair with zeal, and appeared satisfied with what the mirror showed him.

It showed him a young man with brisk, thick hair, a firm jaw, a clean eye and a sardonic mouth. A young man of nippy movements, and with feet on the earth. A young man of fine muscle and good figure. A young man whose expression said he would disbelieve almost anything you told him, because experience and observation of his fellows have taught him that credulity exists only to be exploited. A young man of that age—twenty-three—when the less primitive are racked by introspection; and a young man who had been earning his living these seven years, and was now supporting a home and founding a family; and beholden to nobody but the givers of Work.

When the kettle had boiled he mixed himself a cup of cocoa, and carried it and the candle up to the sitting-room. He drank it while finishing his dressing. When he had put on an old flannel shirt, a stained and dilapidated suit, and a knotted scarf, he was ready for his working day. He had three suits—a working suit, a second-best, and a best; and his new suits passed through the three stages. A working suit did not cease to be a working suit until it fell to pieces.

He raised the blind and looked out, and *grrrrrr'd* at what he saw—darkness, dripping roofs and a floating brown mist.

Having well washed himself, his next step was to make himself dirty again by lighting the sitting-room fire for the missis. When this was well going, he took from the table his bag, containing tea-can and a stout packet of bread-and-butter and cake (his breakfast), reached to a peg for his cap, and set off. But before he left he paused at the bedroom door to do something silly. He thrust his head into the room, saw that Mrs. Wapping was still asleep, and blew her a flirtatious kiss on his fingers. This was part of his morning ritual.

Ten seconds later he was out in that lamplit darkness, part of a procession of Labour towards the District station and the first workman's train. Six o'clock is the hour when his hammer must be lifted to its daily business; an hour when the clerks and the directors and the secretary are still in bed. He was part of a procession of old men, old women, young men and young girls

—all of them cold, some of them with coughs, some of them with rheumatism, some of them with other incipient sickness; but none of them daring to stop off from Work while they could get about. Jack Wapping overtook and passed most of them. He walked with an easy swing, and he had no cough or rheumatism or headache to slow his step. And he had no imagination, or that coughing procession through the darkness might have dismayed him.

At the station he packed himself into a carriage which was built to hold forty and was holding sixty. He greeted a few "sight" acquaintances with a bright nod, and personal acquaintances with a word or two: "Dirty morning." . . . "This cold enough for ye?" There was not much talk in the swaying train. Half-past five in the morning is not the social hour. He held his bag in one hand, and with the other he held a strap and his daily paper, folded at the sporting page. Fifty other men were engaged with papers in equally difficult conditions. The general atmosphere of the carriage was self-enclosure and Grump. An outside observer would have judged that all these people were very unhappy. They were not. They were cheerful people—even those with coughs and rheumatism—and the Grump was not theirs; it was January's and Half-past Five in the Morning's.

When the train reached his station Jack Wapping fought his way out and swung easily up the stairs. In the street he overtook an elderly workmate. "Better put some snap in it, mate. Two minutes to. Don't want to lose a quarter."

The mate was not stirred. "All right 'smorning. Beson's on the gate."

"Ah! Nice chap, Beson."

"Ah! Not like Mathews. Anyone'd think the Works was *his*. Anyone'd think *he* was losing money if we was five minutes late."

"That's right. Lickspittle, him. Thinks they'll take notice of him and give him promotion. As if they cared a damn who's doing the work and who's slacking. They don't know and they don't care as long as it's done. Been with the firm thirty-eight years and ain't learnt that yet. I believe in giving these people what I get, don't you? If they consider me, I'll consider them. If they only give what they're compelled to give, we can do the same, eh?"

They passed the gate-keeper thirty seconds after the hooter had ceased, when the gate should have been shut, and Jack went straight to his shop. There were greetings. "Morning, Joe.... Morning, Fred.... Morning, Jack." Coats came off, and the man at the furnace took his shirt off. Hammers began to swing. The little shed became noisy with a jazz of rings and taps. Across the noise they talked. "What you do last night, Jack?" "Dirt track. Me and the missis. She didn't half get worked up. Wants to go again. What you do?" "Missis thought she'd like to see a picture. So we went to the Palindrome. Jolly good, too. One o' these Gang films. You ought to go and see it." "What you do, Arthur?" "Did a job of work. Repainted the scullery. Two coats. My blasted landlord won't do a thing for ye, though he's supposed to. He knows if he puts y'off long enough you'll do it yourself. He's no fool." "What you do, Fred?" "Went to the Young Russia meeting. You chaps oughta been there, too. You'd 'a heard something. Remember what I said last week about the party leaders? Well, you should 'a heard this chap. It's just what I said. They're all the same once they're nobbled. They're out for——"

Five voices, including Jack's, shouted "Shuhr ... up! Sick o'that stuff."

"But it's right. If you chaps'd only use yer brains and think a bit. You grouse about turning out at five in the morning, and rotten pay, and yet when people are trying to help you, you say Shut Up. Don't even go to the meetings. You're being exploited all round—by your own people as well as the bosses—and ye won't hear the truth. Look at the economic ramp.... Look at the bankers.... Look at the...."

Jack Wapping loosed his voice at full strength. "Oh, shuhr ... up. We get this every bloody morning. Talk about something interesting.'

"I am."

"Well, it don't interest me. I don't wanter get muddled up with that stuff. It may be true, but I got enough to do thinking about earning me living. I got meself and a wife and a kid coming. It's my job to look after 'em. All these *Ideas* may be very fine, but I got no time for 'em just yet. First I got to pay me way. And that takes me all me time, see?"

He was supported by a chorus of "That's right," and this and the eight o'clock breakfast hooter stopped further oratory. Tools were dropped; bags were opened; seats were claimed. The communal tea-pot was handed round and cans were filled. The atmosphere became companionable. Jack studied his morning paper. "Well, boys, what are we doing to-day?"

The question bore no reference to the day's work. Its reference was to horses, and which horses Shop No. 4 should favour with its communal shillings. For four of the day's races they chose a horse, and one shilling (never more than that), subscribed by the six of them, went on each horse. Fred the Red was as ardent in this as any of them.

"There's a good thing for the two-thirty. I had a word about it from the chap next door. His boy's a stable-lad at Newmarket."

Jack Wapping was sceptical. "Yeah? And what'd a stable-lad at Newmarket know about a horse trained at Epsom? Form's the thing you got to look at. Form. Now for the two-thirty I should say——"

The discussion went into committee and was ended only by the hooter announcing the end of the twenty-minutes breakfast. The decision was the daily decision to await the half-past ten sporting editions.

When these arrived, the choice for each race was solemnly made, and Fred collected the twopences and went out to put the shillings on with the bookmaker's runner who waited outside the gates. Once this, the serious business of the day, was done, the shop became a cosmos of Work and a study for any painter who set human beauty above pretty beauty. It showed brown, sweaty muscles, animal breathing, brutal rhythms. It showed the curse of Adam in being. It showed fire and dirt, and the power and fine facility of human hands. The young men of the group, in their rough strength and symmetry, could have passed as the gods of old poems. The old men were patriarchs and carried unflagging old age in its own stern beauty. It made a little epic of energy and skill, gross and splendid.

But Jack Wapping knew nothing about this. He knew that he was at work, which was sufficient to justify him in his own eyes. He knew that he was alive, and that he had this daily job at the forge and earned his living by it, and that life on the whole was pretty good. He knew that there was some mystery about this matter of Life which nobody seemed able to get at, and he felt that it could be left to others to worry about. He was too much *in* it to bother about its mystery, and he wasn't capable of much thought. When he did think it didn't seem to lead anywhere; it only muddled you. There were things he approved and things he disapproved, and that was as far as he could go. He liked his meals and his home and his wife and his half-share of the back garden and his Saturday afternoon football, though he would have liked all these to be a bit better than they were. He disliked all changes. He disliked having to work so hard for such slender pay, and he disliked the Trade Union which helped to keep his wages from going lower. He disliked strikes because they upset the even tenor of things, and because he felt a bit mean about holding out on people—even if they were holding out on him. His ideal life was a life of independence of others, a life of the work he would choose to do with no interference from other people; a life into which he could put the best work of which he was capable. His philosophy was expressed in two words with which he answered all enquiries about his affairs—"Mustn't grumble." And most of his time was spent in doing just that. Grumbling at the weather; grumbling at his pay; grumbling at the price of things; grumbling at the behaviour of other people; and suspicious that everybody and everything were not what they seemed. If you told him that Henry Ford was the ideal employer, he wouldn't believe it. If you told him that Russia was the only country where the worker was honourably treated, he wouldn't believe it. If you told him that the Labour Party was operating for the benefit of the workers, he wouldn't believe it. If you told him that God is in His heaven, and that life is continuous on different planes, he wouldn't believe it. They sound all right, but he knows there's a catch somewhere. There always is in anything that seems good.

But all this was on the surface. Within himself he knew that he Mustn't Grumble; that things might be a lot worse; that he was Rubbing Along pretty well with £2 18s. 6d. a week and a little home and a wife, within limits, as good as they make 'em. He knew that he wasn't a slacker and that he was getting as much money as the next man who did the same kind of work; and with that he was content. There was really very little to grumble about, but to *appear* happy went against his English grain. He used his grumbling as a mask to suggest a doughty manhood which would have nothing but the best.

At the twelve o'clock dinner hooter his hammer fell from his hand and he reached for his coat, and made for the gate. Two of his mates followed him. They went across the road to a restaurant labelled "Old Joe's." Old Joe undertook, in his announcements, to supply "A Good Workman's Dinner, 9d." and usually he did. But his success or his failure brought him the same return—ninepence and grumbles.

Over the dinner—Irish stew and liberal potatoes—they talked little. They did not go to dinner as to a gracious interlude in the day. They did not eat for the pleasure of a harmony of flavours, or for any gratification of the palate. They ate to satisfy a craving hunger, and they did not eat prettily. But when the Irish stew and the sultana roll were done, they talked. They discussed the prospects of Chelsea, and whether West Ham's star man would have recovered from his injury by Saturday. They discussed their gardens. They discussed the manager of their section of the Works. Fred the Red wanted to know why office-workers—even down to office-boys—got their pay during their annual holidays and Bank Holidays and Christmas, while they, who happened to work with their hands, and were the backbone of the Works, couldn't have a summer holiday without losing pay. Was it fair? What was the idea? Why was a clerk so much considered above a skilled ironworker? Was it——? Jack Wapping agreed that it wasn't fair, and went on to talk of the way his missis cooked tripe. A way which would open their eyes. Next time he found a real winner, at a man's size price, they must come round to his place and try it. What about Sunday? Not that there was any pleasure in going out on Sunday. He himself loathed Sundays. Summer wasn't so bad; you could muck about in the garden and do things. But winter ... what was there to do? All these miserable religious people shutting everything up. Just the day when people got the time for entertainment and pleasure they shut everything up. Thought they could make you go to church by doing that.

Well, it'd take more than that to get him inside a church. Why couldn't we have a Sunday like they had in other countries—all the amusements open? And them that was working could have a day off some other day of the week. The very day when millions of people who couldn't travel during the week, could travel to see their friends, was the day the railways cut down their services. Sunday was hell. He wished he could work Sundays and have Tuesday off when things were open. Fred the Red took up the challenge.

"Serves you right. Because you won't organize. You won't attend meetings, even. If you want a free Sunday you can get it. You only got to make a bit more noise than the religious crowd. But all you do is grouse. And when anybody tells you the way to shake off the shackles of——"

"Oh, for Gawd's sake don't start that muck all over again. This ain't Hyde Park. Listen—there's the hooter."

Back in the shop he swung into work. The process of digesting a quickly-eaten and ill-balanced meal robbed him of a little of his morning ardour, but the afternoon held a spot of interest which kept him going. It kept them all going—the speculation as to the fate of their communal shillings and individual twopences. Was that money going Down the Drain, or would it bring them extra packets of cigarettes, an extra something for tea; perhaps a visit to the Dogs? If they came through on two or three races at a long price it would mean a new something-or-other which they had long desired. Naturally this afforded them matter to occupy the mind, and though it was a daily event it came to them freshly each day. Success meant that pleasant prize which appeals to the rich to the comfortable, and the poor; to those who need it and to those who don't. It meant Money for Nothing.

The afternoon's labour was broken by the news of each race. They had backed horses in four races, a shilling on each horse; which meant an outlay of eightpence per man. The result of the first race was given by the newsboy at the gate without purchase of a paper, a courtesy rewarded by occasional drinks. Their employers should have blessed this result; it sent a new spurt of energy through the shop. Their first horse had come home at 100–8. They were safe for the day and Money In; two shillings per man. The other three results gave them no trepidation. If all went down they were still Money In. They gave Fred the Red hearty smacks: the horse had been his choice.

On the second race they were losers, and on the last race they were losers; but the third race set them up for the week. A winner, an outsider, tipped by only one newspaper prophet; and the price 66–1. They congratulated each other on an outstanding day—fourpence out and twelve-and-six in, each of them. It was sunshine and wine to them, and the shop's hum of work had a cheerful note. Employers set upon getting the best out of their men often ignore human nature. They think of swimming-baths, light and airy workshops, gramophones; when, human nature being what it is, they could get the best every day if they would only find winners for their men.

At four o'clock Fred the Red made tea from the communal tea-caddy, and they switched on the lights, and for ten minutes they took a "mike." They returned to labour with zest, and at the five o'clock hooter they were still going strong. But at the first blast tools were flung down, and they stretched and looked for their coats and packed their bags. The firm had no rush of work so there was no question of overtime. Jack Wapping did not like overtime, but he missed no chance of it. He liked his rest and recreation, but overtime pay at the rate of time-and-a-half was worth the sacrifice. This overtime pay he always handed to the missis to put away for her own clothes.

They straggled out into the dark evening, some slowly, some alertly. Jack Wapping shouted an airy "Good night, boys," and "Don't be late in the morning," and "Hope we have another day like to-day," and a few seconds later was well up the street. Work was done. He was a free man and a citizen, soiled and grimy, but sure of himself. He was tired but he did not slouch; his youth wouldn't let him. He walked as sturdily and swiftly as in the morning. In his late 'teens he had been something of a sloucher, but that was because he had few interests—nothing to do in the evenings and only the dull old people to go home to, with their complaints that he should do this and shouldn't do that. Now he was his own man, with a home of his own and a wife to turn to. It made a difference to a chap.

He debated what they should do that evening; the pictures, the local music-hall perhaps, second house. Or there was a sixpenny dance at St. Peter's Hall. Or he might put up those new shelves that the missis wanted at the side of the fireplace. Plenty to do. He debated subtle and amusing little ways of springing the great news about the day's horses—go in with a long face of ruin; or throw the money into the room before he entered; something like that.

But when he got home and went upstairs to his room, these things seemed silly; not the real Jack Wapping. He entered as he entered every evening; casually, the sober Englishman. "Hullo." "Hullo." "Been busy?" "Pretty fair." "What you have for dinner?" "Irish stew." "Good?" "Not so bad. Might 'a been a lot better before it was good. How you been?" "Oh, pretty fair." "'M. Like to do anything to-night? We *can*, y'know." "Can we?" "Ha. Had a good day to-day. Two winners. One of 'em sixty-six-to-one. Twelve-and-six in to-day. So anything you want. . . ." "Well, suppose we save it. I don't quite feel like anything to-night." He became concerned. "Oh . . . er . . . is it?" "Oh, no, just usual." "I see. . . . Well, I'll go and have a wash. Then I'll be able to give y'a kiss—eh? See anybody to-day?" "Mother came in 'smorning to see how I was. And I had a cup of tea 'safternoon with Mrs. Rayne." "Good."

The scullery, common to the three families of the house, was empty. At the sink he stripped to the waist and splashed soap and water over head and shoulders. When he was dry he made a careful shave. Then he slipped his coat over his shoulders and ran upstairs to the bedroom.

Ten minutes later he came out—a new Jack Wapping. Shining face, blue collar and shirt, bright speckled tie, second-best grey suit. He entered their living-room with a hearty and long-drawn "Ha! Feel better after that. Now we'll have a kiss—eh?"

They had a kiss. Mrs. Wapping admired him. She felt that any woman could be proud of him when he was dressed for the evening. "I got herrings for your tea. They're good for you." "Right-o. I dessay I can manage 'em."

He managed three of them and seven slices of bread-and-butter. Over the tea he told her of the day's doings—the job of

work they were on; how they had selected the horses; the latest
outbursts of that pie-can Fred the Red; how old Arthur's kid had
been knocked down by a motor-bike. . . . When he could eat no
more he helped the missis clear away, and while she washed up
he went to the "easy" chair with a cigarette. It was not a very
easy chair; most of its springs were gone; but with a couple of
cushions it wasn't so bad. Like the rest of the home, it was an
oddment, battered and fourth or fifth hand. They had picked
up their home in junk shops and in the street market, but it was
their home. Nobody could take it away; it was all paid for. He had
seen enough of young chaps furnishing with new furniture, and
unable to keep up the payments, and having it taken away from
them, and sleeping on the floor. That wasn't his idea of the way
to start life. Battered stuff his, perhaps, but all paid for. The only
new article in the room, which stood out in its newness, was the
clock presented by his mates of Shop No. 4.

He sat with legs stretched out, relaxed, approving his home,
his wife, his condition and life generally. This was the best part
of the day. He thought if Fred the Red was set as *he* was set he'd
probably have no time for his crackpot ideas.

After half an hour of this alert reverie, which was as near as
he ever got to thinking, he shook himself. "This won't do." He
got up and fished in a corner behind a cotton curtain for a tool-
box. The rest of the evening he spent in making and fixing three
small shelves for the little alcove on the other side of the fireplace,
and chatting amiably with the missis while working. By half-past
nine the job was done, and the missis agreed with him that he
had made a Proper Job of it. They debated whether it should be
stained green or brown, and decided on green as lighter. Jack
would get the stuff and do it to-morrow evening. She went downstairs to get his regular supper—cocoa and cake.

He took his supper in the easy chair, drowsily. Twelve-and-
six was on his mind. "Twelve-and-six," he said, with a wink.
"Twelve-and-six in, old girl, eh? A few days like this every week,
and we'd be on velvet, eh?" "Time you went to bed, Jack. You're
half-asleep now."

"You're right." He got up and made preparations for the morning, and Mrs. Wapping began to pack his breakfast. On all nights

except Saturdays ten o'clock was his bedtime; and six hours' sleep was necessary to his energetic frame, and he could always have slept longer.

In bed in the darkness, with his young wife and coming child beside him, he thought over the day and over things generally. He was keeping his end up. When you have paid rent—eleven shillings for two unfurnished rooms—and Trade Union sub. and Health Insurance and Unemployment Insurance and Slate Club and Weekly Workman's Ticket, there isn't a lot left out of £2 18s. 6d. to meet the rest of life with. But though Friday afternoon (pay day) usually found them down to a penny or twopence, they were doing it. How they did it he didn't know, but they did it in defiance of all the scientific theories of the economists and of those amateur philanthropists who lay down schedules for working-class families. He was keeping his end up, and that was enough for him. The condition of England, the rigid laws of trade, the meaning of money—of these things he knew nothing. The looming object in his life was Work, and he had got Work. If God had asked him if there was anything he now wanted his only answer would have been—an easier job and better pay. As he sank into sleep there was nothing that troubled him but the missis. He wondered when her time would be coming. He hoped it would be all right. Accidents happened sometimes. An awkward business. It gave him a little tremor.

He was still thinking about it when an interval of drowsiness interrupted him; and the next thing he consciously knew was that the alarm clock, set for half-past four, was delivering its call to arms.

ONE HUNDRED POUNDS

Granpa Ben lived in a crowd, but he lived alone. He lived alone because he wasn't much liked and didn't try to be. He suffered —or said he did—from a number of complaints, and was eager to make them vocal. He sat every morning at his cottage door in one of those little rural patches which one finds here and there enclosed in London's labyrinth. It was a patch of scattered cottages with long gardens, and a couple of small fields bare of grass. All around it the metropolitan fever ran, but never penetrated to it. It was quiet, bedraggled, and forgotten. There, at his door, he would sit every morning delivering his *appassionata* to any who would listen. They were not many, and they did not listen long.

Scarcely anybody went into his cottage. His only regular visitors were the woman who cleaned it each morning, and one other. This was the one person who could put up with his old-man egotism, his old-man ways, and his old-man talk. His young grandson. It is rare for the young to tolerate the old, even when they are pleasant, but young Bertie not only tolerated Granpa, but appeared to like him.

Granpa Ben didn't think very highly of the human race, but whenever he let himself go on that topic—and he often did—it was understood that the human race didn't include Bertie. The human race didn't give up their Wednesday evenings to sitting with the old man and telling him the local gossip. The human race didn't come in and nurse him when he was sick. The human race didn't come in on Sunday afternoons and read the paper to him. For the human race he had only a grr-cha. For Bertie he had only benedictions.

Bertie was the one person he could trust. He didn't think much of his youngest daughter, whose son Bertie was. He didn't think much of his elder brother. And he didn't think much of his other daughter, or of any of her children. Bertie was the only one he cared for and the only one he wanted to see. Bertie was the only one who paid him any attention in a way that looked as though he liked paying him attention. The others, when they had done it, had done it perfunctorily. They were free, so far as Granpa Ben was concerned, to go and hang themselves; and he had told them so. They were a rough lot, and he didn't trust them.

Of course, when a distant and still older relative of Granpa's left him his life-savings, amounting to one hundred pounds, some of them came round to see him. He expected they would, and he had spent the afternoon in preparing for them various rounded, if not polished, phrases. They did not stay long. Before they had time to congratulate him he told them that none of it was for them and they needn't waste their time smelling round for any of it. They were a rough and stupid lot, and they hadn't done anything for it, and would only waste it. When he (Granpa) was gone, it was to be all for Bertie, and he would make a will that very night. Bertie was a nice, quiet lad who would handle it sensibly.

Their reception angered them, and the announcement, a sort of pendant to the reception, dropped pepper on the anger. They went away with a few of the best soldiers' farewells to Granpa, and with much bitterness towards Bertie. Among themselves they said things about Bertie; the kind of thing that disappointed legatees always say about the favoured one. Bertie, they said, had known what he was up to. Bertie was a sly one. Bertie must have guessed there'd be something to come into. Bertie and his Wednesday evenings and his reading the paper on Sundays. Urrch. . . . They expressed the hope that the old man would make a mess of his will so that it would be set aside. One or two expressed the hope that he would peg out that night before making the will. They expressed hopes about Bertie in terms which no modern novelist has yet found an excuse for printing.

When Granpa went up to the lawyer's office to collect his inheritance he demanded the company of Bertie. At the lawyer's office he demanded his money in cash. Cheques, he said, didn't look like money, and he didn't trust them. Bertie said that a cheque would be better, as he could pay it straight into a bank or into the Post Office. Granpa said he didn't want no banks and no Post Office; he could look after his own money. Bertie said it was dangerous to keep money in the house—as much money as that

—particularly in the kind of place where they lived. The lawyer, too, said it was dangerous, and advised cheque and bank as the safest and most usual. Granpa told them both to mind their own business. All his life he had kept his bit of money under his hand, and it was as easy to keep a hundred pounds as it was to keep a few shillings. If people wanted to rob you, they'd rob you for a few shillings as certainly as they'd rob you for a hundred pounds. The lawyer said that wasn't his experience. A hundred pounds was a concrete sum with potential uses. With that sum a person could get away, could go abroad out of danger, and still have some of it left for beginning a new life; whereas a few shillings meant nothing but a few petty purchases. The one was a definite temptation to any violence; the other wasn't. Granpa said the lawyer's experience was limited. Many robberies had been committed for the sake of a few beers and cigarettes, some of them with violence, and one or two with murder. But the lawyer needn't worry. Anybody who was going to get Granpa's hundred pounds would have to be a smarter man than Granpa; and anybody who was going to murder him to get it would have to be tougher. He doubted that such people existed.

So he carried his hundred pounds away with him in a little packet of notes, and, despite Bertie's exhortations all the way home, he said he was going to keep it in his cottage. Under his hand, so that he'd always know where it was. So Bertie, like most other people who argued with Granpa, had to let him have his own way. When they got home to the cottage, the old man took the packet from his inner pocket, and put it on the mantelshelf. "Well, there it is. And it's going to be yours, me boy. But it's not going to stay there for long. I'm going to find a home for it, what nobody else'll find till me will's read. . . . Yes, Bertie, that'll be all yours when I'm gone. Sit down, me boy. We've had a tiring day. I think we deserve a little drop o' something hot." So they had the something hot, which was cocoa for Bertie and rum with a slice of lemon for Granpa. Granpa kept looking at the mantelshelf, and nodding. "Yes, it'll be all yours, me boy, when I'm gone, and I hope you'll see that none o' them others get any of it. They're a low lot. Of course, you won't get it yet awhile, y'know. I'm not going out yet."

Bertie said, dutifully: "I certainly hope not, Granpa."

"No, me boy. But you'll be a bit older by the time I do go, and you'll appreciate it more. You'll be able to put it to better uses."

Bertie said, "Yes."

"I don't believe in people having money too young," the old man went on. "Not even when they're as steady as you. Later on, you'll thank me for minding it for you."

Bertie agreed, and said that later on he would know more about the business which interested him—the business of newspaper and tobacco shop—and would certainly be better able to use the money to better advantage. But he again urged his Granpa to put it into a bank. Granpa said no, he wouldn't. Bertie urged that, sleeping alone in the house, he was open to all sorts of attack. People would hear—indeed they already knew—that he had come into money, and might take a chance on his having it in the house. He ought to have somebody to sleep with him. Granpa said he didn't want nobody. Bertie said that with the rough lot around them, anything might happen. Granpa thanked Bertie for his concern, but said he could look after himself. Perhaps Bertie might keep a look-out on his way home, and if he saw anybody suspicious about, he might see what they were up to, and if necessary he could warn his Granpa. But apart from that, he needn't worry.

So Bertie went off, though with no sign of not worrying. Granpa locked the door after him, bolted it, and set the catch. Then he went back to his living-room, and sat down to his final night-cap.

For some time he sat in that pleasant state of mazy reverie which he would have described as "thinking things over." There was a certain gratification in being in possession of a hundred pounds. He didn't want it himself; his needs were few and were covered by his pension. The gratification arose from the fact that it annoyed so many people. To annoy people usually involved some tiresome activity; here he was annoying quite a number of people without doing anything. He was chuckling at the image of their annoyance when his ears half-caught a sound—a baby of a sound which he couldn't be sure was a sound. At first he thought it was such a sound as would be caused if somebody had touched ever so lightly the latch of the door. Then he thought it wasn't. It was probably the shredded sound of a cold cinder cracking, or of the fork slipping down the rim of his supper-plate.

Ten seconds later he had forgotten about it. He sat in drowsy comfort, wondering what he should have for dinner to-morrow. He thought of sausages and then he thought of roast lamb. Still wondering, he passed one or two stages towards the edge of sleep when he heard, and heard clearly this time, a little sound which wasn't the same as the first sound but was no more natural or friendly than that sound. It was the sound which is made when a boot touches gravel and sharply draws back. He sat up then. He reached to the lamp and turned the wick low. He sent his being into his ears, and became nothing but a listener. But after a second or so all he could hear was drumming silence. He heard it so long that finally he ceased to hear it because it was everything. A sudden movement of his hand as it scraped his trousers to still an itching on the knee had the effect of a buzz-saw.

Some seconds after the silence had recovered from the scrape of his hand and was again in possession of the room, his being passed from his ears to his eyes. Something beyond the doorway of his living-room had moved. He was so keenly listening at that moment that his eyes were not properly reporting to him. They reported only that they had something to report. He called them into action, and began to look. He looked over the back of his chair, and as he looked he located the movement. He looked into the little entry which came between his living-room and the door. It was in darkness; the dim light of his lamp did not reach it. But though it was in darkness it was not in such complete darkness as to make movement imperceptible.

The latch—the latch of his front door—was moving. It was moving without sound; a gentle up and down; once, twice, three times. Then it rested. It was as still as it always was, and for a moment he couldn't be sure that he had seen it move. But in the succeeding moments he knew that it had moved, and that he had heard those noises, and that the noises and the movements were connected. Also that the two details meant a burglar or burglars. Somebody, as Bertie had said, who had heard about his money and was working on the chance that he might have it in the house.

All right. If that was their game he would join it. He sat still, and watched. His eyes then received another movement; a much clearer movement this time because it had a white covering. It was the movement of the forepart of a hand coming through the little letter-slit and feeling for the middle bolt.

Confronted with this intelligence Granpa proceeded to action. He got up. Despite his age and those infirmities he was always talking about, he got up without a sound, and when he got up he had the poker in his hand. With old-man movements but young-cat stealth he crossed the room to the dark entry. He stood aside from the door, keeping his breathing as subdued as possible. He bent down and listened. Somebody, he was certain, was on the other side of the door, listening, too. For some seconds the man inside and the man outside crouched and listened and waited, only a wooden board with lock and bolt separating possible murderer from possible victim.

Then, when Granpa knew from the feel of his skin that somebody with no love in his heart was outside that door, he made two soft movements. He slipped lock and bolt, and opened the door. A crouching figure darted back but not swiftly enough to escape Granpa's third movement, which was a downward sweep of the poker. The figure went down with the poker. Granpa saw it down, and ran back to the parlour for his lamp.

In his haste he wasn't as quick as he wanted to be in turning up the wick. His hand was shaking. When he got to the door with the light the figure was still there, but it was not alone. It had been joined by another figure. A young girl was bending over it. He recognized her—Mary, Bertie's special friend. "Why—Mary—what's all this? What you doing here?"

"It's Bertie."

"Bertie? Good God, what've I done? I struck him down. Bertie? Good Lord; I thought it was the burglar, and I struck him down. He must 'a been coming to warn me, or chase 'em off. I asked him to keep a lookout going home. He kept telling me to be careful. He must 'a chased 'em off just as I come out. Why couldn't I 'a copped them instead of him? And now I've struck him down, and perhaps—— Oh, God."

Mary snapped at him. "It's all right, it's all right." She had one hand on Bertie's wrist, feeling his pulse, and the other on his head. "He isn't dead. He's only stunned. Look—he's coming round." The old man dithered round her with "That's good, that's good." She waved him off. "Well, don't stand there doing nothing. Silly! Go and get some water. And a cloth. He'll be all right in a minute. But get some cold water—quick."

She kept her hand on Bertie's wrist till the old man had gone inside. She was a nice girl, and she wanted to spare the old man the sight of the knuckle-duster and the bit of wire which had slipped out of Bertie's sleeve.

THE MAN WHO LOST HIS HEAD

The accident that befell Peter Smothe was no such accident as is met by compensation from our popular daily papers. Their catholic and imaginative lists stop short of that kind of accident.

It is said of many of us when, in times demanding the packed thought of an hour, we are unable to attain even a moment's reflection—that we have lost our heads. The term is one of those passionately tropical images which fall so glibly from the lips of accountants, stockbrokers, cricket-umpires and other repressed poets. But with Peter Smothe the thing happened. He did actually lose his head, and lived to know that he had lost it.

It began in that restiveness which comes to many a man at fifty. He came to see his life as flat and unprofitable. He looked about him and saw—or thought he saw—other men leading vivid-coloured lives; lives as full of zest and effulgence as a fire-opal; while his own had been safe, warm—and dull. He was fifty, and he had had none of that highly-charged life of which he read in the newspapers. He forgot, of course, that they were they, and he was he; and that a man cannot choose his way of life. He can be only what his chemistry and his karma allow him to be. He can be only himself. To seek to be something else is to throw the whole mechanism of his being out of gear.

But Peter Smothe was sick of being himself, and at fifty he decided to be something else; anything else. He felt it a sorry thing that a man's life should run on one set of rails. That a man should spend his little span in being but one kind of man—a soldier, an actor, a geologist, a scholar, a lawyer, a painter. Why couldn't he have a little of each? He realized that at fifty it was too late to try for a little of each, but at least he would have something different. He had had enough of his rails, and since most of his life was gone, this was the time, if ever, while he was yet able and healthy, to try something new; something utterly alien to his previous experience.

So, upon a fine morning, he packed a small bag, and left his Kensington flat without any word of his intention; and was never again seen in it.

He had no clear plan, other than escape into a new world. A passing delivery van gave him his first pointer. He saw the words "Pentonville Road," and he hailed a taxi, and said, "Pentonville Road." He stopped the taxi half-way up the long ascent of that road, and went down a side turning. There he took the first turning on the right. He walked down this littered street, studying its decrepit houses. One of them, not so decrepit as the rest, had a card in its window—"Lodgings for a Respectable Single Man." He knocked at its door, and when it was opened he crossed the threshold of that house and of his former life.

*   *   *   *

In that street he remained for four months. He was within a threepenny bus-ride of his own home, yet, after a week or two, as far from it as if he were in Iceland. He became one more of the annual hundreds of Mysterious Disappearances.

And he became a new man. He ate in squalid little eating-houses. He hung about the Islington streets and talked to all sorts and conditions. He consorted in bars with the less-favoured specimens. He learned to use their talk, and do their things, and soon to accept their thought. He told himself that he was having a high old time. He looked back on his staid bourgeois life with impatience and contempt. To think of the years he had wasted on it. He wondered how he had endured it so long. He wondered why he had looked with shivers on the kind of life he was now leading. He gave his old self a grimy laugh.

He felt that he was now leading the real Bohemian life; not the well-to-do imitation of it; and realized that it was the life he had always, secretly, wanted to lead. His friends, he thought, would call it *going to pieces*. He himself called it *branching out*. He thought of the anecdotage with which he could surprise them when the mood took him to return. He thought of the wisdom by which he could shock the innocence of two of them, who claimed to know things because they dabbled in social service. He did not know that he was not going back.

There came a night when he met, in an obscure tavern near King's Cross, a man from whom he would have shrunk a few months ago, but whom now he saw as an Interesting Man. The creature was dark-haired and untidy; his face and hands were so unclean that they gave dreadful hints about the rest of his body. He wore a tattered overcoat with the collar turned up. The collar was buttoned and the rest of the coat hung from him in a fork. He used the unclean hands to stress the keyword of every sentence in a way that suggested the Near East. He, too, was about fifty, but he had led a more tumbled life than Peter Smothe, and his face was lined and drawn. But the eyes were brighter and more alert than Peter Smothe's. They had been called to look upon strange and unexpected things in their fifty years, while Peter Smothe, until four months ago, had seen little that was strange and unexpected. He still had, in moments of repose, the calm eye of the club-man.

The stranger, having selected Peter Smothe for his audience, began to talk of things he had seen. He revealed not only alert eyes but a brain. It was not the kind of brain Peter Smothe knew in Kensington and in his clubs; but he would have been disappointed if it were. The man talked of really strange things, and talked of them as casually as men talk of a visit to the theatre. He talked of The Power. He talked of the *Petit Albert* as others talk of the latest novel. He talked of the sword and the cup, and of things he had seen done in Greece.

"Mind you, I don't talk in this way to these people here. It would be a waste. But you, sir, I perceived at once, are an educated man. You think. These people"—he waved the soiled hand and the funereal fingernails—"these people—cattle—dross for cemeteries. Impossible to talk to. But you, I see, think things out. You are not bemused by such childish nonsense as laws, and such artificially-created things as crime. Dope—don't you agree? All dope. When I see the way that tenth-rate little humbugs in power bemuse the mass of the people with their stale old tricks, I could——" He finished on a crescendo of profanity.

Peter Smothe hugged himself. "Most interesting man," he thought. "Lovely Type. Quite like one of these master-criminals." Aloud he said, "Won't you have a drink with me?"

"Don't mind. Make it a whisky and peppermint." When the drinks came he said, "Suppose we sit down. Could you pull that other chair over to this table?" Smothe went over and fetched the chair. The soiled hand shot into the pocket of the soiled overcoat. The soiled hands carried the glasses to the table. The hand that held the glass of Peter Smothe went back to the overcoat pocket. "Now we can talk. . . . My views perhaps may seem extreme to you, but often to reach the desirable middle it is necessary to exert ourselves towards the extreme. There was a man I knew in Greece. An extraordinary man. You'd have liked him. Satan we called him. I learned a lot from him. Oh, a lot. Not all I wanted to learn, or I wouldn't be in this place talking to you. But enough to be useful from time to time. *His* views I used to consider extreme, but I found he was only aiming farther than he wished to reach. Which is what I always do. I remember once in Marseilles, when I was in some little trouble——"

Peter Smothe repeated to himself that This was Lovely. He was in touch with the real underworld of which he had read in novels. This man, talking a farrago of street profanity and sham education, good phrases and illiterate phrases, was a Find. He decided that he must cultivate him.

After a return of drinks they parted on Peter Smothe's suggestion that they meet the next evening. The stranger thought it likely that they would. He could not be sure; affairs might detain him; but he hoped to be there. If not, some other night. As they went out Smothe trod on a tiny empty capsule which lay by the stranger's feet. He did not notice that he had trod on anything.

He walked to his dingy room in a queer state of elation and fatigue. The man's appearance and talk had elated him, but something else about the man had exhausted him. It was as though he had sucked all vitality from the air about them, and left Smothe only the nitrogen. His head was light and his legs were heavy. It was a clear, dry night, and still early—just the night for one of those prowls in dim quarters which had become a habit with him. But he found that he wanted only to be in bed. The ten-minute climb from King's Cross to that bed called for an effort. It seemed unattainably distant. Every hundred yards seemed a mile. But after some hours of plodding he made it, and was surprised to see that his clock showed that he had left King's Cross twelve minutes ago.

*   *   *   *

His first awareness of himself next morning was that he was a living Thirst. He could not realize arms or legs, or life itself. His whole being was Thirst, and his only sense-perception came through the throat. He got up to seek water, and drained three glasses. Within a few minutes his mind and body resumed the normal coursing of life, and he felt able to wash and dress.

Having washed and half-dressed, he prepared to shave, and it was here that the normal coursing of life was again arrested, and his being became one extreme sickness. He had just taken up the shaving-stick, and had tilted the mirror, when he dropped the shaving-stick and almost knocked the little mirror to the floor.

The face that looked back at him from the mirror wasn't his.

He had tilted the mirror in the casual faith that it would show him what it had shown him throughout every day of all his years —a chubby pink face, a little blond moustache, blue eyes and thin blond hair. What it did show him was black, lank hair, a lined and drawn face, dark, restless eyes, a black forecast of beard, and a general air of grubbiness.

Wondering whether it were nightmare, or if he were still suffering from last night, he rubbed his hand heavily across his face, and looked again. There was no doubt of it. He was awake; from the street came the cries of the morning; from below came the familiar sounds of that dingy house; from the window he saw the bedraggled figures he saw every morning. And in the mirror he saw a face that was not his.

Before he understood the full implication of what had happened, and the frightful dilemma in which it placed him, he was aware only of that sickness which comes to all men in presence of the unaccountable. Something had happened which *didn't* happen; something out of nature; something against the sun. We live by a peaceable faith in the course of nature; a faith which takes so much for granted that if the morning sun were to shine upon us from the west, and the stars appear in daylight, we should stand still in dismay. For the moment Peter Smothe stood still in dismay. Four times he went to the mirror, and four times he sat down and stared at the carpet. The impossible thing *had* happened. He had a new face. The rest of his body was the body he had known for fifty years. His hands and legs, which he examined slowly and in fear, were his. The face was not.

At the fourth examination of it, he felt that, strange and repellent as it was, he had seen it before. He spent some minutes in trying to remember where he had seen it, and only after searching about all the queer faces he had seen in the last few months did he recall last night. The Interesting Man in the bar. And then he recalled the unusual effect of two glasses of light beer. The face he saw in the mirror was the face of the Interesting Man.

When, in the course of an hour, he came to consider his position in relation to everyday affairs, he realized that he could not face the woman of the house. He would be a stranger. He would be a stranger everywhere. One thought came to him; the thought that comes to every man in every kind of disaster. Flight.

At eleven o'clock when, as he knew by custom, the woman was out, he fled. He took his bag and fled, and boarded the first bus that came along. He sat in the bus with the desolate feeling of being Nobody. His light pretence in leaving home and sinking his identity under an assumed name was now changed to dismal fact. He was not Peter Smothe, and he was not really the Interesting Man in the bar. He had achieved completely what he had thought he wanted: he had got away from himself.

He left the bus at the Strand, and took the bus behind it, which was labelled for Waterloo. He did not know why he should go to Waterloo, but he decided that he might as well go there as anywhere else. It was distant from Islington and from Kensington, and it was a quarter which, outside the platforms of its station, was known to nobody of his own sort.

In a dim street off Lower Marsh he found a room to let, and into it he took his misery. He hunched himself on the narrow bed, and tried to realize what had happened, and to follow out its implications. But the thing would not resolve itself into thought; he could only look at it and wonder. A wild hope came to him that as this mad thing had happened, so it might un-happen. It might last only for a while. Whatever madness was at work upon him might exhaust itself, and he would find himself again Peter Smothe. He thought of his Kensington flat, and prayed that the thing might pass, and that he might be again Peter Smothe, and abandon his foolish antics of the last few months. Every fifteen minutes he went to the mirror, but the mirror had nothing for him.

Towards late afternoon his feeling of sickness increased, and he realized that he had eaten nothing. With an effort he dragged himself out to seek some secluded eating-house. But he went no farther in his search than some twenty paces.

He had scarcely left the house when two men confronted him. They confronted him very solidly, one on either side of him. The stouter of the two said, "Just a moment. We are police-officers. What's your name?"

"Er—what—er—Peter—er—Arthur Exford."

The man studied him. "You answer to the description of a man wanted by the Southampton police. Known as Boris Gudlatch."

"That's not my name. And I've never in my life been in South-ampton."

"I see." The officer looked at the poor street and the shabby creature, and seemed trying to reconcile the street and the shab-biness with the delicate voice. He made his decision on the street and the shabbiness, and took Peter Smothe by the arm. "You better come along to the station. If there's a mistake we can soon settle it." He turned to his companion and nodded towards the house. His companion went to the house, and Peter Smothe was taken to the station.

At first he was bewildered and incoherent, as all respectable men are when their arms are taken by policemen. He could not clearly grasp what was happening, or why, or what he should do. He could only utter feeble protests. At the station he was told that he must expect to wait awhile, as officers were coming from Southampton with witnesses. If a mistake had been made, he would no doubt understand that the interests of justice must be served even at inconvenience to innocent people. He contin-ued to protest. "I don't know what it's all about. I've never been in Southampton in my life, and my name isn't the name you mentioned. I'll admit that it isn't the name I gave." Under this new trouble he forgot the trouble that had come upon him in the morning. There was no mirror in the station, and he talked to them as himself. "No. It isn't the name I gave. I had a private reason for giving that. Nothing to do with anything that would interest you. I've just been going about London seeing life. Actually, my name is Peter Smothe. My address is Helsingfors Mansions, Kensington. You'll find me in the telephone book. And you can ring up and ask my man to come along."

"You were there yesterday?"

"Er—no. No, I wasn't there yesterday. I haven't been there for a month or so. I told you I've been wandering about London. But I left my man enough to go on with, and he'll probably be there."

"Well, we'll ring him up."

They rang up, and they told Peter Smothe that his man was coming along by taxi, and had expressed some anxiety concerning the disappearance of his employer. The officer, not certain whether he had an amiable eccentric, or a bluffing criminal, gave the benefit to courtesy, and assured him that if he were the man he claimed to be, everything would be all right, save for the inconvenience, which couldn't be avoided.

Within half an hour his man arrived, and he got up from his hard chair with a gasp of relief. "Hendrick!" Hendrick took no notice. He turned to the officer, "Where's Mr. Smothe?" The officer said, "There." Hendrick looked round the room. "No. That's not him." Peter Smothe became indignant. "What's the matter with you, Hendrick? I *am* here." Hendrick looked again at him. "Don't know what you're talking about. You're not *my* Mr. Smothe."

"But I *am*. Hendrick—my parrot—Mulvaney. You know the parrot, Mulvaney. And my collection of enamels. And the cabinet in the corner with the Bohemian glass. Hendrick!"

The officer looked at both of them. Hendrick looked at the officer and indicated Peter Smothe with a nod. "Seems to know a lot about Mr. Smothe's habits and his flat. But that ain't Mr. Smothe. I been with Mr. Smothe eleven years. I ought to know him. He went off sudden-like some months ago, and I haven't seen him since. But that ain't him. My Mr. Smothe was yellow-haired and pink. Chubby face, sort of. Blue eyes. Always very neat and what you might call spruce. *That's* no more him than I am."

"But, Hendrick——"

Hendrick was thanked for coming, and Peter Smothe was left alone. He was left alone for half an hour, which gave him time to realize his folly in sending for Hendrick. The impossibility of explaining to Hendrick that though he had lost his head he was still Peter Smothe. The impossibility of explaining to police-officers that a man could lose his head, and go about with a head that didn't belong to him. The impossibility of explaining anything.

And then his loneliness was broken. Four other men came into the room. They were ushered in by an officer and they sat down on chairs, gingerly and self-consciously. An odd lot. A man who looked like a clerk; a man who smelt of fish; a man who looked wicked enough to double-cross Satan; and a man who couldn't look anything because his eyes were everywhere and his face was constantly changing. The only point they had in common was shabby appearance.

They had had only the time to look round the room and grin or grimace at each other when a big man came in and presented a young girl to the company. She stood in the doorway and looked them over one by one. The big man said, "Well?" Without hesitation she pointed to Peter Smothe. "That one." "Sure?" "Absolutely. Wearing different clothes, but the face is unmistakable. I saw it quite clearly when he stood in the light before he started running." "Thank you." He called through the door: "Take Miss Jones to the next room. Don't let her see the young man. Then send the young man."

A young man came in. He, too, studied the company. The officer lifted his head in enquiry. The young man nodded. "Yes—over there by the window. That one." He pointed to Peter Smothe.

"Sure? He says he's never been in Southampton at any time."

"I'm certain that's the man I saw. Different clothes, but the face —I saw it quite clearly for some seconds. Don't see faces like that every day. Not in Southampton, anyway."

The young man was waved out, and when he was gone the four other men in the room were waved out. The officer turned to Smothe.

"Two witnesses have identified you as a man wanted by the

Southampton police. I hold a warrant for the arrest of that man, known, among other names, as Boris Gudlatch, on a charge of murder."

"Mur——"

"It is my duty to detain you and take you to Southampton to answer a charge of robbery at a jeweller's shop in Humstrum Street, at five o'clock yesterday afternoon, and of murdering John Smith. It is my du——"

"But I tell you again I've never in my life been in Southampton. It's ridiculous. It's rubbish. These people are making a mistake. I——"

"You are at liberty to make a statement, or not; as you please. If you wish to make a statement, it is my duty to warn you that anything you may say may be used in——"

"I've not been out of London at all the last four months. I was in London all day yesterday. I was wandering about all the afternoon, and I can call witnesses who saw me at nine o'clock near King's Cross, and——"

The officer had held up his hand, but it wasn't the warning hand that made him break off. It was the realization that he had spoken to nobody through the whole afternoon, and had stopped nowhere; and the realization that a man could have been in Southampton at five o'clock, and yet have reached a King's Cross bar by nine o'clock.

"If you don't wish to make a statement," the officer said, "it would be better to say nothing for the present."

So Peter Smothe said nothing. He saw the utter futility of making a statement. He saw the impossibility of an alibi, and the idiocy of telling this man, or any men, that somebody took his head away last night and gave him his present head in exchange. He closed his mouth and dropped his hands, and suffered himself to be taken to Southampton and confronted with three more eye-witnesses.

Six weeks later he learnt his lesson. He learnt in exaggerated form what every man learns in some degree who commits his kind of folly. He learnt that when a man wilfully flies from his life; when he wilfully loses his true self—or his head—he has lost it for ever.

MURDER UNDER THE CROOKED SPIRE

The apt setting and circumstance for the successful murder are manifold. Some assassins, with unconscious fitness, choose violent settings for their deeds of violence. They take their "prospects" to riversides at midnight; to subterranean caverns; to unvisited hilltops; to forlorn cliff paths, or to the dreadful hollow behind the little wood. Others, not so violent, choose quiet settings for their quiet devilry. They take their "prospects" to unoccupied villas in demure suburbs; or they work in the peace of domesticity, and so respect that peace that they disturb it with no harsher weapon than a helping of weed-killer from the garden-shed. There is, indeed, no end to the settings which, by their fitness for purpose, connive at and collaborate with the evil that men do.

But none, I think, could be more apt than that chosen nearly a century ago by Mr. John Platts of Chesterfield, the city of the Crooked Spire, for his solitary excursion into evil. For Mr. Platts pursued his daily affairs in circumstances which were ideal for murder; circumstances which surely offered a constant temptation to murder. He was so placed that throughout his working hours he was surrounded by blood, and could appear in public at any time of a working day with blood on his hands or on his clothes without exciting the least tiresome conjecture among his fellows. Queer noises and the sound of blows could arise in his shop and no neighbour would attach sinister intent to them.

Mr. Platts was a butcher and kept a slaughterhouse.

He was a young man of twenty-two, squat, bull-necked, and only five feet tall; and had been engaged for a year or so in this business before he saw its potentialities in the matter of settling old scores. When he did realize this, he put it to the test, and very nearly committed the successful murder. It was a murder that would have satisfied the Master, who, in his essay, laid down once and for all the requirements of a murder which could be considered as a contribution to this Fine Art. It would also have satisfied the amateurs of his imaginary Club, and would have notably stirred that connoisseur nicknamed Toad-in-the-Hole. It did, in fact, for almost twelve months, rank as one of the many success-ful (*i.e.,* undiscovered and unsuspected) murders of England, and would have passed into the long but uncompiled catalogue of these disasters, but for the sanitary zeal of the owner of a court-yard in which was a pond used as a public shoot.

I say "zeal" because a hundred years ago, sanitary attention to public places was not given daily or even weekly; often not at all. The man who was responsible for discovering that there had been a murder stated that he had been frequently employed by the owner of the yard to empty that particular pond; "fre-quently," as it appeared in evidence, meaning once a year. Mr. Platts had doubtless counted on that pond remaining as undis-turbed as other ponds on private property; and it was only the perverse and unpredictable factor of a landlord's annual concern for public health that brought him to the gallows.

The murder was discovered late in 1846, and Mr. Platts was tried and condemned in 1847. But the deed was done in 1845.

At that time Mr. Platts was running his butcher business at Chesterfield—it was situated in The Shambles—in partner-ship with a man named George Collis, destined to be his victim. Collis, a young man of twenty-six, apparently financed the busi-ness, and sometimes financed Mr. Platts; and the sole motive of the murder was that Platts owed his victim some two or three pounds, and the victim was pressing him for the money. A motive that may sound frivolous for an operation so profound and irre-vocable, until we remember that in the past many a murder was committed for less than that sum.

At the beginning of December, 1845, Mr. Platts decided that he must find a way out of his three-pound trouble. Accordingly, on December 7th, which happened to be a Sunday (a sad slip on the part of Mr. Platts, since that choice of day fixed in people's minds certain things which, coming on any other day, they would have ignored): on December 7th Mr. Platts made an appointment with his partner that they should meet that evening at the shop of a mutual acquaintance, and he would settle. George Collis accepted, and in the half-lit murk of that December evening, while the godly were stepping to worship at church or chapel, he set out to keep the appointment, blessedly unaware that he was keeping an appointment with Death. At the same time Mr. Platts also set out and, to the accompaniment of church bells, made *his* way to the appointment, which, in his case, was an appointment with Murder.

This was no crime of impulse; it was planned and the mutual acquaintance at whose shop they were to meet—a man named Morley—was in the plan. He, too, owed money to Collis; and it was agreed that Platts and Morley should jointly dispose of Collis, and by this act evade payment of their debts, and benefit from whatever plunder the pockets of the victim might afford. And there was a shadowy third, unnamed in the report of the trial and indicated only by asterisks, who appears to have been brought in by the murderers in case their joint assaults were ineffectual. He played his part in the affair, and at one point of the proceedings was seen by several people but not recognized.

People saw, indeed, though obliquely, a great deal of this business. The odd thing about it, that marks it from most murders, is that it was a murder committed, so to speak, under everybody's nose. Nobody *saw* the murder, and nobody at any time saw a corpse; but many people *heard* it. Heard it distinctly; heard blows and a fall and heavy breathing. But they heard these sounds from a slaughterhouse, and naturally none of them guessed what actually was happening. Only the fact that it was a Sunday caused them, as I say, to note certain goings-on in The Shambles, and to remember those goings-on some nine months later. But at the time of noting them they only chaffed Mr. Platts on his Sabbath activity, and murder was undreamt of. When at last it was discovered, not a spot of direct evidence could be brought against Mr. Platts. The evidence upon which he was arrested, tried, and ultimately condemned, was cumulative and damning enough, but it was purely circumstantial.

*   *   *   *

At about a quarter to seven of that Sunday evening of 1845, Mrs. Franks, of the Angel tavern, near The Shambles, had in her public parlour two regular customers—Mr. Collis and Mr. Platts. From their talk it appeared that they had on this occasion met by accident, and were on their way to another meeting-place. They chatted amiably and drank with each other, and at seven o'clock went out together. At a little after eight, Mrs. Franks again saw Mr. Platts, but this time he was alone. Mr. Collis never again visited her tavern.

At ten minutes past seven a young carpenter, named Heath-coat, was passing through The Shambles when he heard voices coming from a shop which he knew to be Morley's. The door was open and he looked in. He saw Morley, Platts, Collis and another man—the shadowy third—whom he did not know. From their tone and attitude they were disputing. It sounded interesting, and he stood aside to hear more of it. But he was disappointed. It seemed that one of them had heard footsteps outside, for, just as the dispute was reaching a point of excitement, the shop door was banged and barred. He went on his way and thought no more of the incident.

At half-past seven a young man named Slack, on his way to his usual Sunday evening drink and talk, saw two men support-ing another, who appeared to be very drunk. His legs kept giving way. He recognized one of the men as Platts. He saw them arrive at Platts' shop, and saw them push the drunken man inside. He saw the man fall down, and he heard the door being bolted and saw a curtain fixed over the ventilation holes of the door. Judging the affair to be the end of a binge, he, too, went on his way, and thought no more of it.

A few minutes later, a man named Harvey, a friend of Platts, was passing the shop when he came to a sudden stop. The shop was in darkness, but he heard a sound of blows—blows deliv-ered on something soft. "What's Jack Platts up to," he thought; "killing a calf on a Sunday?" He waited a few seconds, and was rewarded by hearing a human noise—long and loud breathing, as of one in pain. He was on his way to a house opposite, the house of some people named Bellamy, with whom Platts also was acquainted. Knocking at their door, he told them what he had heard and wondered whether Platts were ill. The two Bellamys and himself went to the shop and knocked, and stood in the dark street listening. Only a wooden door separated them from the terror within.

"Art tha ill, Platts?" they asked. "Art th' alone?"

To which Platts, whose voice they recognized, answered, "Ay. I had some rum at the 'Angel,' and it turned me queer. I'll be all right soon."

"Wouldn't tha like a light? Shall us bring some water?"

"No. I'll come over in a minute."

They went back to their house, and told a guest, a Mr. Kirk, about the business. Platts had for some time been "walking out" with Kirk's daughter, Hannah. Mr. Kirk appears to have been a lively and facetious fellow. He put his own interpretation upon the presence of Platts in his shop on a Sunday. He, too, went across to the shop and hammered on the door. "You, Platts—open the door, tha little beggar. Th' ast got my Hannah there." The answer was silence. Mr. Kirk then threatened to break down the door and get Hannah out, and upon that Platts opened the door and stepped out to the street. Kirk tried to push past him, but Platts pulled the door to. Kirk said, "I'm going to have her out." Platts said, "She isn't here, James. She's at church, and I'm going to meet her when church is over." Kirk then demanded what he was doing in his shop on a Sunday, and Platts explained that he had some meat left over from Saturday, and had come to let a little air into the shop.

They left the shop together, and went across to the Bellamys. Kirk noticed that Platts had a long scratch on his left hand which was bleeding. "How didsta get that?"

"Caught it on a meat-hook when I was opening ventilator. I'll get Mrs. Bellamy to dress it."

The Bellamys noticed that he was in a rather agitated mood, but put it down to his sickness. He went to the kitchen to wash his hand, and Mrs. Bellamy bandaged it for him, and Mr. Bellamy gave him a drink. They talked of this and that, paying little attention to what was said. When, in the course of talk, Platts said that he had heard of a raffle at Mansfield for a watch, and was going to put in for it, they forgot it a minute after it was said. But it came back to them nine months later.

After his drink and a rest, he got up and said he would go and meet Hannah coming from church. On the way he made his second call at the "Angel," where Mrs. Franks noticed his bandaged hand.

"Now what's tha been doing?"

"Caught it on a meat-hook."

"Ah, that's nasty. Tha'll have to be careful of that, case it festers."

The "Angel" was the house to which the bell-ringers of the near-by church repaired when service had begun, and Platts was accustomed to spend his Sunday evenings in their company. But this evening he did not stay long; he excused himself by saying that he had to meet Hannah, and he left them, and met Hannah and took her to her home.

While he was doing this, Mr. Holbrook, proprietor of an eating-house, was sitting in a tavern in another part of the town waiting, with his best patience, for his friend George Collis, who was already half an hour late. He had seen him at half-past six that evening, and they had appointed to meet at this tavern at nine o'clock. It was then half-past nine, but Mr. Holbrook waited; in small provincial towns appointments partake a little of Spanish appointments; they are seldom kept to the dot. He waited till ten o'clock; till half-past ten; till eleven; till midnight. Still no George Collis. At that he gave it up and walked home. His way took him through The Shambles, and past the shop of John Platts. He was surprised to notice a light in the shop and to hear sounds of things being moved about. He tried to look in but found that all apertures were covered. Like all the rest, he went on his way and for a long time thought no more about it.

It is a common notion that the chief characteristics of small-town life are curiosity about neighbours, and that unmathematical game called "putting two and two together." Curiosity the people of The Shambles did display, but it was momentary, and none of them bothered his head with doing sums. Each of them saw a little or heard a little that Sunday night, but none of them, save one, saw enough or heard enough on his own account, to lead him to suspect anything deeply wrong. And as the majority of them did not come into contact with each other, there was no opportunity of pooling notes. Not until the trial were all the isolated and unmentioned observations of some ten witnesses added up. When they were they made a most conclusive sum.

From that Sunday evening George Collis was no more seen or heard of. The young carpenter Heathcoat, who saw him in Morley's shop, was the last person to see him alive. He also saw what *had been* Collis, but remained ignorant of the nature of what he had seen. On the Monday evening he was waiting near The Shambles to meet his brother, who lived in a different part of Chesterfield, when he was attracted by the movements of three men. His brother came up just then, and he drew his attention to them. "Look—there's Jack Platts and Morley. Don't know who the other chap is. Wonder what they're doing." They saw three men creeping through the darkness with a bundle about five feet long. The bundle appeared to be heavy; at every few yards they rested. The brothers watched them carry their burden into a spot called Bunting's Yard, where the big pond was. "Wonder what they're doing," the first brother repeated. "They look a bit queer."

"Oh, nothing. Happen they're just clearing out some offal from their shops. Taking it down to field to bury it."

They turned away, and did not recall the little incident till nine months later, when it made one more point against Mr. Platts.

During the week Mr. Platts was noticed to be in possession of a pair of laced boots, different from those he usually wore; also he had a watch. He did not claim that this was the raffled watch. When it was remarked upon, he said he had bought it from a local character known as Lanky Bill. (But at the trial Lanky Bill, from whom the defence, for reasons of their own, forced an admission that he had been in prison and lived with two prostitutes, denied that he had sold anybody a watch. He had never had a watch to sell.) Mr. Morley was also noticed to be paying off some small debts which had been running some time. He appeared to have plenty of loose silver.

After a week or so, and towards Christmas, people who had missed George Collis from his usual resorts, and who knew that he was in partnership with Platts, asked Platts if he knew what was become of him. Mr. Harvey asked him, and Platts said he had probably gone to Manchester. He added that he would like to see him, as he (Collis) owed him five pounds. To another enquirer he said he had heard that Collis was in Macclesfield. To another he said he had seen him outside the town driving a chaise.

Still no suspicion rested upon him save in one mind—the mind of Mr. Harvey. Mr. Harvey was given to thinking, and he had his doubts about the goings-on of that Sunday evening, and did not refrain from uttering them. More than once he said to Platts: "Jack, I could have sworn you had somebody in the shop." On each challenge, Platts denied it; but Mr. Harvey was not satisfied. He even went so far as to utter more than doubt, and Mr. Platts came up against the utterance. A blacksmith with whom he did business spoke of it in the course of casual conversation. "Jack, there's strong suspicion that tha murdered somebody on Sunday."

"Who says so?" asked Mr. Platts, not at all perturbed.

"Tom Harvey."

"Arrr . . . Reason he suspects me is because I was in me shop on a Sunday letting air in, and fell over lantern and cut me finger."

As the months went on even Mr. Harvey seems to have shed his doubts, and soon George Collis was forgotten by all save his mother and his fiancée. In those days disappearances of young men from small towns were common. It was a time when people could move about freely, and did. Strangers came to a place from nowhere and natives disappeared into nowhere, and nobody asked questions. A man could travel unrestricted to any European country, and could take any job in any country for which he was fit; and Europeans could come freely to England. There were no passports; no barriers against "aliens." Also, it was a peak period of emigration. America and Australia were wide open; and many a young man, restless under his daily routine, walked out of his home without warning, to appear later in Australia and not to reappear in his home-town for perhaps twenty years, if ever. Families were used to this, and if one of the young sons disappeared it was assumed that he had "gone for a soldier," or shipped as a sailor, or gone to "foreign parts."

But in August, 1846, light was given to many people to see what they might all along have seen and what only Mr. Harvey had seen.

One morning, towards the end of that month, Mr. Valentine

Wall was busy cleaning out the big pond in Bunting's Yard when he found his work obstructed. By the aid of pitchforks he and his assistant found that the obstruction was a number of bones and a saturated coat and trousers. This conveyed little to Mr. Wall; he assumed that the bones were cattle bones, thrown there by the butchers, and that the clothes were cast-off clothes carelessly got rid of at the most convenient spot. He put them in a truck, and told his assistant to shoot them into a dust-pit in a near-by field. But the assistant had another look. He noticed that two of the bones had coloured garters round them, and that the articles of clothing, when put together, made almost a complete outfit. Only the boots were missing. As a dutiful citizen, and to be on the safe side, he reported the matter to the police. The police came and saw and summoned a doctor. The doctor declared the bones to be human bones, of a man between twenty and thirty. He found on the front of the skull three deep fractures.

Enquiries were now set about, and when the story became known, Mr. Harvey, Mr. Bellamy, Mr. Kirk, Mr. Heathcoat, Mrs. Franks, Mr. Slack and some others recalled the mysterious vanishing of George Collis. They recalled that he had last been seen on a Sunday evening of December, and Sunday evening recalled to them a particular Sunday evening marked by curious goings-on. In the taverns round The Shambles they began to talk. When the bubble of talk had subsided a little and cleared itself, all the events of that rainy Sunday evening began to crystallize around a scratched hand out of business hours, and a pair of boots and a watch. Some of them went to the police. The police went to the mother of George Collis.

She told them that she had last seen her son on the afternoon of December 7th of the previous year. When he left her house he was wearing a black surtout, canary-coloured waistcoat, brown trousers and black neckerchief. The neckerchief bore his initials. He always wore laced boots and stockings, and with the stockings he used one white garter and one red garter. He had with him a canvas purse and a watch. All this, save boots, purse and watch, corresponded with the clothing found.

While the remains were being removed by the police, watched, of course, by all the inhabitants of Bunting's Yard, Mr. Platts passed by. One of the crowd, a woman, spoke to him. "They say it's the body of George Collis. Dosta think he did it himself?" To which Mr. Platts answered that he had last seen Collis on a Saturday of December, when Collis had two razors with him and "threatened to make away with himself." He forgot, apparently, that razors don't cause fractures of the skull, and that he had been seen with George Collis in the "Angel" on *Sunday* evening.

Next day an inquest was held upon the remains when some, but not all, of the evidence in police possession was given. In addition to the evidence of the "Sunday night" witnesses, the police also had evidence that Platts had on two occasions offered for sale, and later had pawned, the watch he had acquired soon after December 7th; a watch which had been recognized as once belonging to George Collis. The evidence offered at the inquest, meagre as it was, proved sufficient, however, to make one person very ill. On the day the inquest was closed the man Morley was taken with a fever. Two days later he died in delirium.

With the evidence, published and unpublished, in their possession, there was nothing for the police to do but to arrest John Platts. He was arrested early in September. He was tried in March of the following year. He was hanged outside Derby gaol on the morning of April the First.

It was a clear case from the beginning, but one little puzzle remains; the puzzle that gives the story its special interest. It is that shadowy third. Who was he? Why was he allowed to remain at liberty and anonymous? Why did Platts shield him and, in the confession he wrote in the condemned cell, represent him by asterisks?

THE LONELY INN

The tall man on the lawn outside the cottage gave the cottage a long look and nodded at it. "Seems to be a perfect week-end cottage. Just big enough for us and easy to run. Ought to have some good week-ends here."

The man with him agreed. "Yes. Hasn't got everything but almost everything. Good view from the lawn. Stream over there. Woods on the left. Even the house-agent must have strained his Arabian vocabulary in listing it."

"Yes. Village quite interesting, too. People seem a bit surly, though."

"You must give country people time. We've only been here two hours, remember. Maybe the soil's got something to do with it. Certain soils make cheerful people; others make taciturn people, or hot-tempered people."

Their wives appeared at the cottage door. "Why don't you boys go and explore a bit? There's nothing to do in here. The maid's left everything. We've only got to heat the soup. Dinner'll be eightish."

The tall man said, "Right." And then to the other—"What about it, Mac? Shall we stroll and see if we can find the local?"

Mac nodded, and they went through the gate into the lane. To the right lay the village, a mile away. They had seen it an hour ago. They turned to the left. The lane here was little more than a grass-track. By its width it appeared to have been at one time a road, but now its surface was rough grass corrugated with wheel-tracks. The grass in the ditches on either side was of somewhat stronger hue.

It was a winding lane, and at no point did it disclose more than a hundred yards of itself. The hedges stood high, and afforded no view of the surrounding country. "Almost like a shrubbery," the tall man said. "Wonder where it leads to eventually, and whether we've got to come back the same way." They followed its bends for some minutes, and then the tall man said "Ha!" explosively. And then: "The oasis. I see a sign. Let's hope it isn't a desert mirage. But I'm sure I saw a sign, just over the hedge-top." At the next turn he gave his friend a facetious pat. "There we are! Thought I wasn't mistaken. As we're in Derbyshire they ought to have some of the real Derbyshire ale. Step out, my lad."

The inn's exterior was somewhat weatherbeaten; almost uninviting; but it was an inn. It had known no paint for some years, and its door and windows had a bedraggled aspect. The door and its stone front bore brown and black patches. It showed a faded sign of "The White Cockade."

The two men paused. The tall and talkative man said, "H'm. Hardly one of the picture-postcard inns. But that's no fair test. All its good points may be inside. I've found several like that. Anyway, it's the only one, so. . . ."

They went in. They found the inside no compensation of the outside. They entered a dim and silent tap-room. It contained the usual fixtures of a wayside public-house—old wooden benches, old wooden trestle-tables, an old and wide fireplace with the ashes of the last fire of winter, and an old and strong smell. Nothing in the place was grey in colour; yet it offered a general feeling of greyness. The landlord, standing listlessly behind the stained bar, was a man of heavy features and sunless eyes. The very type of man who ought not to keep an inn. His physical appearance accounted for, if it did not explain, the air of lost-heart and letting-things-go which hung over everything. One light, a shaded lamp, lit a small pool about the bar. The rest of the room was a muslin of shadow which gave common objects an uncommon shape.

They ordered their drink, and the landlord served them without "Good Evening" or other word. The beer was good. They drank, and looked about them. It was then, when their eyes, fresh from the bright evening, had become adjusted to the half-light, that they noted a slight stir among the shadow. Looking more closely, they saw that the room, which they thought was empty, held company. Some half-dozen dim figures sat along the benches and on chairs. No two sat together. They sat at intervals, each self-enclosed. They were men of ordinary appearance, in soiled or ragged clothes of miscellaneous quality and style; but their silence and their attitudes made them extraordinary.

The horrific figures evoked by the lobster nightmare or the unchaining drug cannot so freeze the human mind as the sight of the ordinary creature in the extraordinary attitude or state. De Quincey's picture of the fat man of Keswick sitting alone on his lawn in shirtsleeves on a bitter March midnight brings more of the authentic recoil than any of his laudanum visions.

And so these dumb and solitary figures affected the two visitors more than any scene of ugliness or violence. Something in their peculiar arrangement suggested that they were sitting like that with some reason. It was as though they had placed themselves like actors on a stage, awaiting the rise of the curtain. The silence of the place, whose silence was underlined by the intermittent drip-drip of the beer-tap, also had an effect, and when the talkative visitor wanted to say something he found himself muttering.

He touched his friend. "Queer place, Mac." The other nodded. "Must be a side-entrance somewhere, I guess."

"Why?"

"Well, I didn't see anybody come in, but a minute ago I'd have said there were four people in the far corner."

"So there were."

"Well, there's six now. And there were two just behind us."

"Yes."

"There's three now."

Mac looked about him, and found that his friend was right. He found, too, that the company, without moving, was exchanging signals. He saw a head nod, and then another head respond to it. He caught his friend's eye, and together they watched the invisible message pass visibly along the room in nods. It was as though a row of Victorian mantelpiece images had been set in motion. All these people, it seemed, knew each other; yet sat apart holding no communication beyond nods.

He brought his earthenware mug sharply to the counter. He expected it to make in that silence a startling report, and had made the motion deliberately in the hope of bringing a touch of life to the room. But somehow, possibly by the shape of the room, it made only a faint noise, and the company ignored it. His friend turned to him: "Wonder if there's a deaf-and-dumb institute near here. And if this is Founder's Day." He looked at the landlord. "Customers not very talkative," he said. The landlord continued to stare at nothing. He looked at Mac, and they exchanged a smile.

It was while he was taking a cigarette from the packet held by Mac that he became aware that the silence was being very gently troubled. At first he thought it was the swishing of a curtain. Then he knew that it was a whisper. A whisper was passing along the benches and chairs, and once or twice he caught its burden. *That's him. That's him.* He saw that Mac had heard it, too, and as they turned and looked at the benches they found the dilapidated faces of the company fixed on them. It seemed to him, as he turned, that they were fixed on him, but with the next glance he saw that they were all looking beyond him, at Mac. The moment they saw that they were observed, the faces dropped, and each man resumed his former pose of looking at his knees.

Mac picked up his mug and finished it. "Fit?" His friend nodded. They stepped out of twilight into orange sunset and scented fields and limpid light. They took some six paces from the inn; then the tall one stopped and said, expressively: *"Gawd!"* He took three deep breaths. Then: "I'd like to show that place to some of those literary blokes who write about the old village inn, and the mellow company, and the rich rustic voices, and Uncle Tom Cobleigh and all."

Mac agreed. "Still, we can't have everything. The cottage is about perfect, so we shall have to put up with the local. But what a hole. And not merely dull and dingy. Something more than that about it. We must investigate again. A place like that in this gorgeous country must have a reason for being what it is. Some story behind it. And why were they so interested in me?"

"Lord knows. Don't look as though they could be interested in *anything*—let alone an everyday specimen like you. Perhaps they'd seen you in the village, though, and were thinking of giving you the village greeting—'arf a brick."

"Huh. . . . Well, I've found some queer pubs in my ups-and-downs of England, but that's the queerest so far."

*   *   *   *

The next day, Saturday, they spent in a motor-run of exploration, and got back to the cottage between six and seven. After a little pottering, Mac said, "Coming down to the lousy local?"

"Not this evening, I think. I've got about four or five letters I want to answer, so's to have to-morrow free. You go."

"Right. I'd like to have another look at it. Something about it fascinates me. It had the feeling of something going to happen."

"Don't be long, though. I've got an appetite. Don't want to have to wait dinner."

"Needn't worry. I've got one, too. I'll be on time."

Mac stepped out of the door as the other settled himself at a table. As he passed the open window he heard his friend call, "What's the date?" He answered, "April thirty," and swung down the lane.

And dinner was late. They waited until twenty to nine, and then, as Mac had not returned, they waited no longer. "I suppose he's managed to get the deaf-and-dumb school talking, and can't tear himself away. He'll have to have what's left, and have it half-cold. Ethel can't go down and drag him out. Create a bad impression on our first week-end—wives pulling husbands out of pubs. 'Father, dear father, come home with me now.'"

Ethel was dealing with soup. "Oh, he'll turn up when it suits him. He's done it before. When he finds an interesting local, as he calls them, he forgets time."

But he did not turn up. They left the door unlocked until one o'clock; then, as he had not turned up, they went to bed. "If he turns up now he'll have to throw gravel at the window. Gone off on a binge, perhaps, with one of the deaf-and-dumbs, and staying the night. Probably turn up with a hang-over about church-time to-morrow."

But he did not turn up. He did not turn up at church-time or at any other time. The trio left at the cottage never saw their Mac again.

At about mid-day his friend went out to look about, and to enquire at the local and in the village. Just outside the gate he met the old man whom they had engaged to keep the garden tidy during the week.

"Morning. D'you happen to have seen anything of my friend?"

The man looked at him dully while the question sank in and wandered through his mind to pick up some association with "my friend."

"Your friend?"

"Yes; the man who came with me. You saw him yesterday."

"Ar—'im. What would he be like?"

"Stocky figure. Red hair. Horn-rimmed glasses."

"Oh . . . 'im. No. I ain' seen 'im. I remember 'im. Scotty, I says to meself."

"Yes. He is a Scot. Well, he went out yesterday evening—down to the inn here—and was coming back in an hour. But he didn't come back last night. Nor this morning. I wondered whether you'd seen him or heard anything of him."

"No-o. I ain' seed 'im."

"I was just going down to the inn to ask if he'd been there. Thought perhaps you might have been there last night and seen him." He went into the lane and turned to the left. The man stopped him.

"This way, sir."

"No. This way. The inn's down here. Down the lane."

"You mean up the lane."

"I mean down the lane."

"You mean up the lane. The 'Green Man,' just outside village."

"I don't. I mean down the lane." He pointed to the left.

The man stared at him. "Dinno of no public down there."

"No? I see you don't know your own country. Often happens that the stranger finds what the inhabitant misses." The man looked puzzled. He stroked the stubble of his chin. He seemed about to say something but didn't say it. He was dealing with a Londoner. Queer things, Londoners. Said what they didn't mean, and twisted words about, and called it wit. Played silly games called *pulling your leg.* Sometimes they weren't quite right in the head. Zanies, some of 'em. This seemed to be one of that sort.

"I dinno of no——"

"Ah, but I do. I'm just going along there to ask if my friend called in last night. If you care to come along I'll show it to you. And you can sample the brew."

"I'll come along with ye, but——"

They went along. They went down the twisting lane. The gardener held his puzzled expression, but made no remark. They went along until they came to the elm, through whose branches the sign had been visible.

"Just at the next bend," the tall man said; and they made the next bend. Having made it he looked about him. "Funny. Must have been the *next* bend." They went on and followed the next bend, and this bend marked the end of the lane and its junction with a main road. The tall man now did some staring. "Well. . . ." He looked back up the lane. "Can't have *passed* it, can we?"

"No, sir, we din pass it."

"I remember it as just this side of that elm." He took a few strides up the lane. "Yes. This side of the elm. Just opposite that gap in the hedge. I could have sworn that—— And I'm certain we never left the lane. But if so, what the devil——"

The gardener watched him with blank expression. He appeared to have no interest in the proceedings. He was humouring a Londoner. The tall man turned to him. "Well, if it wasn't in the lane where was it? How did we lose ourselves? You——" Then something in the man's blank face arrested him.

"There bent no public in this lane. Nor anywheres bout 'ere. Nothing bout 'ere for four miles. Not till ye come to the Golden Lion. And that be along the road—four mile."

The tall man stared at him and then at the lane, and then shouted. "But man, we did come to a pub here. We did have drinks in it. In the lane. A dismal place."

The gardener looked sad and shook his head. With rustic civility, or polite contempt, he refrained from comment. He repeated only "Bent no public in this lane."

"But, man, I tell you——" He broke off. He realized that he could not insist on the fact of his pub, because nowhere in the lane was there any pub. There had been a pub, and now there wasn't a pub. He strode backwards and forwards. "What's happened here? What funny work's going on here? We can't both have been insane. We did come to a pub here, and we did have drinks. What do you make of it?"

The old man stared at the horizon. "If there'd been a public 'ere I'd 'a known it, I come down 'ere twice a week. Never no public 'ere in my time. Nor in me faather's time. But I do remember me granfer telling me that 'is granfer told 'im there were a public down 'ere."

"What!"

"There *were* a public down 'ere. I do remember me granfer telling me that 'is granfer told 'im it were burnt down. It were mixed up in sommin in 'istry. Nigh on two unnerd year ago. I dinno the rights of it, but 'e did say sommin' 'bout some kind of war. And a lot o' Scotties come 'ere. And one of 'em sold the others. And the people set fire to the place, and they was all burnt. 'Cept the one that sold 'em. And 'im they cursed with their dying breaths."

THE WATCHER

The dim little shop stood at the corner of two dim streets of a North London suburb, far away from the main road. It stood alone in a world of little houses, and its air was forlorn and dejected. It was closed now, and its blinds were down, but even when it was open it looked little less forlorn. It seemed to have no self-respect; to be only perfunctorily a shop, and the people who kept it clearly didn't care whether they kept a shop or not.

That sort of shop in bright and busy surroundings is dismal enough, but this shop, set alone at a corner of a street that was gritty, ill-lit and empty of people, seemed at the last gasp of depression. It was so ordinary, so much a replica of thousands of other lonely corner shops in dim streets, that it spread a slow stain of foreboding on the evening.

It even sent a touch of this foreboding to the shabby man who was approaching it. He was approaching it on definite and urgent business, and was anxious to reach it and get the business done; yet, as he came nearer to it and saw its face, his step hesitated and he regarded it with dislike.

He was approaching it on a quest for money. It is odd how much money can be found in poor streets. Thieves go for big houses, where there is little but marked jewellery and plate, when, if they only knew, many a house in a dim back street is as valuable as any of the big houses. The stuff is more easily to be got at, and it is in negotiable and untraceable form—silver, gold and Treasury notes. Stories of people who mistrust banks and keep all their money in their homes often appear in the news, and each known story may be taken to represent fifty unknown. One might say that in every poor street there is at least one house with a good hoard.

This little corner shop had one, and the fact of it was not un-known. It was known to the shabby Mr. Roderick. He had known of it long ago, but until lately the knowledge had been knowledge

only, with no personal meaning for him. The fact that they kept a
large store of money in that place was merely an item of interest
like learning that the Browns had another baby. But now it was
more than that. Mr. Roderick's circumstances had changed, and
with them Mr. Roderick himself had changed.

To the new Mr. Roderick that knowledge was an asset; it could
be applied to his problems. The statement that knowledge is
power is true, but only if you know how to apply one particular atom of your million atoms of knowledge to a particular
occasion. Mr. Roderick had done so. In the thrall of a particular occasion he had suddenly netted out of the pool of his mind
the particular atom of knowledge, which could lift the thrall. He
wanted, urgently, to cross the sea, and it was while searching for
the means of the journey that recollection came to him of the
little shop he had known so many years, and its secret bank of
which, by accident, he had become aware. He had not seen it for
six months, but a quiet visit the day before had told him that it
was still kept in the same haphazard way by the same haphazard people. And a little quiet watching this evening had assured
him that they still followed their weekly custom of going out in a
group every Wednesday evening.

He had watched them go, and had counted them. He knew
their usual time for returning, and felt that he was safe in assum-
ing that they would keep to it. It was a time that gave him leisure
for the job in hand. He could go at it without a rush. He didn't
feel like rushing it. It might be more difficult than he thought. He
didn't like the look of the place, somehow; seemed to be something "wrong" with it, though he knew it was all right. He sent
a glance up the dark street each way; then shook his shoulders,
slipped out of the doorway that had sheltered him, and slipped
over a wall to the back entrance.

And then he was there, working at a window. He worked
swiftly; he was familiar with the windows of that district. He
was also familiar with the back entrance, and many a time in the
past he had stood at the back door and talked to members of the
family. Within less than a minute the window was open, and he
was slipping through it. All his movements suggested something
slipping.

Once inside the house he stood stock still. He knew how to stand still, so still that all his nerves were at rest, his muscles motionless, and his breathing imperceptible to anybody within two feet of him. He stood like this while he counted up to a hundred. Then he began to move across the room to the door.

Had you been there, you would not have seen him move. You might have seen him at one spot of the room, and then at another spot; but you would not have seen him move. The darkness was no barrier; he knew this room; he went across it in three shots.

The stock-room, the little room behind the shop, was the room he was after. He slid across a section of the passage, and reached it. There was a door to open, but he dared not risk a light in the passage. He turned his head aside, and looked at nothing, and used his fingers on the handle. He put all his being into those fingers, and they turned the handle without the tiniest shred of sound. And they pushed the door quarter-inch by quarter-inch, until there was sufficient space for him to pass from one darkness to a deeper darkness.

He was in the stock-room. Here he switched on his electric torch, holding it close to the floor. He glanced round the room. It was much as when he had last seen it; piled with wooden crates, biscuit tins, cardboard boxes and packing-straw. He looked keenly at the disused fireplace and noted that none of the crates covered or obstructed it. He could get at it without risking the noise of moving anything. He crept across the floor and turned the torch into the chimney. He ran his fingers over the bricks of the right-hand recess. As they touched a certain brick his breath ran out softly. The hiding-place was still in use.

He turned the torch upon that brick and with delicate fingers began to edge it out. The movement produced no sound, and he had made no sound in entering the place; the empty house was enveloped in a cloth of silence. Yet when the brick was half-way out his hand dropped, he switched off the torch, his easy body stiffened liked a cat's, and he shot round and faced the door.

He faced only blackness; yet, though his ear had heard noth-ing, his sense had warned him of something—a step, was it? Or a movement of human lips? Or the unclasping of a human hand? He stared into the blackness, listening with all his body; and the repulse that the shop had seemed to give him when he first came to it was repeated. It was like a presence.

But, keenly as he listened, through all the senses, there was no sound, no sound at all. It must have been a little flick of loose wallpaper, or the dropping of a speck of plaster, or the settling of a bundle of the packing-straw. The house was, as he had known it would be, empty. It must have been one of those things, or just his own nerves. He turned again to the stove.

But the house was not empty. There was another man in that house who had also thought it empty, but who was now doubting. He had heard nothing, but he, too, was aware of something, and was also listening with all his body. He did not move from where he was; he just listened. And Mr. Roderick, with his hand on the disused stove, only six yards away from the unseen listener, also listened. These two listened for each other, but while one listened and stood still, the other listened and went on with his work.

Softly the first brick came out, and softly the second. And then the third. Not a sound came to the unseen listener; yet he knew that somebody was there and at work.

When the fourth brick was out, Mr. Roderick flashed his torch into the cavity and saw his reward. Three flat tin boxes. His other hand entered the cavity, and the boxes went from the cavity to his pocket so softly that they seemed to fly in. A fat envelope completed the hoard, and that, too, flew in. Then, still with soft movements, he replaced the four bricks, and stood up.

It was as he stood up that he had again, and this time more powerfully, the sense of a presence. But he had done his business, and could not now bother about the possibility of there being somebody in the house. He had done his business undisturbed, and he must now bother about getting out. He turned to the door, holding the torch well downwards, and then shot back to the stove and lifted the torch.

The torch, shining on to the floor, had shown him a pair of slippers and the lower part of trousers. The torch, lifted, showed him an erect, old man standing against one of the crates and steadily gazing at him.

He knew then that the man had been there all the time; had

seen all his actions; had seen the transfer of the hoard; would be able, since he'd worked by the torch, to describe him. For two, perhaps three, seconds they stared at each other. Then, as he realized his situation, Mr. Roderick's right hand went to his breast pocket, the torch went out, and a life-preserver crashed on to the man's head.

The man went down with a muffled bump. The crate went with him and its fall shook the floor. And at that Mr. Roderick lost control of things. The episode—the strain of the burglary itself, the sense of being watched, and then the discovery that he had been watched—had shaken him. He switched on the torch and rained blow after blow upon the body on the floor. He was still striking when he became aware, not merely of a presence, but of noise.

A noise of men in the passage. And then a noise of men at the door. And then a noise of men in the very room. And then they were on him, and two of them were defeating his struggles and had him down and helpless.

One of the men said, "My God! It's poor old Gregory." And another said: "Why? Now why kill the poor old chap?" And another said: "Look—he's been at the stove. I wonder what for?" And one of those holding Roderick and running through his pockets said: "That's what for—see?" And held up the fat envelope. The first man said: "Yes, but why murder?" And turned to Roderick, and repeated, "Why? Why on earth did you want to kill a poor, harmless old man? So unnecessary. Why?"

Roderick snarled at him. Then said: "Because he'd seen me, of course. I had to. Or I wouldn't have had a chance. He'd been watching me at it. I had the torch on, and he had a clear view of me. Could have described me and identified me. I *had* to quiet him."

The man gave him an odd glance. "You seem to know where they kept their money. Which is more than I do, though I live next door. But you haven't been here lately, I reckon. Have you?"

"Not for some time."

"Ah. I see. That explains. If you had, you'd 'a known that this poor old chap—their uncle—had come to live with them. And you'd 'a known that he's stone blind."

EVENTS AT WAYLESS-WAGTAIL

You might have thought he had taken a dislike to the green wall-paper of his book-room. In a casual moment he had raised his eyes from his desk to look at nothing. Having raised them he kept them fixed on the wall before him. He bent forward from his chair, elbows on desk. He was seeing something more than a green-papered wall. He was seeing a murder.

Visions came to him at day-time as easily as dreams come to ordinary people at night. Always they carried their own touch of the peculiar. They were never of the immediate present. All of them were set some little distance ahead. Usually they were pointless. He would be sitting alone, or walking in the garden or in the street, and between him and whatever he was looking at, there would flash a scene or an incident in living miniature. A country road, and a man, sharply defined, bending over a car. A crowded restaurant in a foreign city, and three particular people at the nearest table, quarrelling. Two lovers walking in a busy street. A man going up the steps of a club, and slipping on the top step. Things like that.

If the time were winter, his vision would usually be related to next spring. If it were spring he would see some moment of the following autumn. With each picture, which came vivid and clear as life itself, there was always some detail, such as state of the weather, flowers, a calendar, which gave him the period; often the very day and hour. He could seldom make anything of these glimpses of futurity, and paid little attention to them. Why, when they had no personal significance for him, they should thus visit him, he could not guess. He assumed, casually, that some shutter of perception which, with other people, remained sealed was, with him, loose, and so at moments would let in a random flash of the time-stream. He let it go at that, and usually forgot the visions in the moment of their fading.

But the present vision was something different. It was a vision to which he must attend, and upon which, perhaps, he might be able to act and be of service. There was murder being done, and it concerned recognizable people in recognizable circumstances. Both scene and figures were strange to him, but the detail was so exact that if ever he could see that place and those people in life, he would know them. That was why he was staring so intently, trying to fix the essential points on his visual memory.

The vision had opened with a view of a village; an English village straggling round a green. There was a duck-pond on the green, with white railings round it. The houses dotted along the green were cottages and villas. Some of the cottages had thatched roofs. Most of the villas had whitewashed fronts and green doors, and little covered balconies. Judged by the flowers in the gardens and the foliage of the trees, the period was early autumn, and the fall of the thin sunshine indicated mid-afternoon.

He saw it as clearly as though a model of the village had been designed and set in mid-air before him. But this model was alive. The boughs of the trees were waving, the bright clouds were moving, and the ducks were paddling round the pond. Even as he was absorbing the scene, human life came into it. A man of about thirty, in sporting tweeds, came from one of the larger houses, with "Avoca" painted on its gate, and moved along the green towards a house next to the church; a house bearing the name "Cranford." He carried a newspaper and looked into it as he walked.

Stern could see the paper and its headline. It was the *Morning Mercury*, and its date was September 3rd of that year; three months distant.

The man stopped outside "Cranford," opened the gate and went up a little garden path bordered by red stone. Along one side of the house was a lawn, a continuation of the lawn at the back, and as the first man entered, another man of about fifty—an energetic fifty—came from the house to the lawn. He was of large figure, erect and grey. He carried a serviceable hammer, and went towards a patch of broken fencing. This he began to nail up. He hammered the nails fiercely, and his actions and the set of his body implied that he would do everything fiercely. As the younger man approached, he appeared to hear his step, and he turned. The glance he gave his visitor was not too cordial. They did not shake hands. They stood for some moments on the lawn in talk, and Stern got the impression that their talk, though not quarrelsome, was on the edge of it. Then the elder man indicated the door and went into the house. The other followed him.

Stern next saw the hall of the house. It made a small square. At different points were golf-clubs, tennis rackets, thick boots—all the litter of the hall of a country cottage. The walls were decorated with old engravings. On a small table was a copy of that day's *Times*. It was dated September 3rd.

He saw the men stand in the hall some paces from each other. He saw their brows darkening and their lips thrusting. He saw the elder man point at the younger, and make a contemptuous movement with his hand. He saw the younger man's jaw shoot forward. He saw him take a quick step towards the other. As he moved, the elder man swung up his arm, still holding the hammer. The younger man came on, the other sidestepped, and brought the hammer down.

He saw the younger man crumple to the floor like a dropped pillow-case. He saw the other drop the hammer, and go down on one knee. He saw his face dark-red at one moment and at the next chalk-white. He saw him fumble over the body and raise the head. He saw him put his hand on the pulse and then on the breast. And he saw him get up with eyes that held pain and dismay.

And then the space between him and the green wall of his book-room was vacant. The vision was gone.

*   *   *   *

For some minutes after it was gone he sat staring and thinking. When he moved it was to reach for paper and pencil, and set down every detail of what he had seen, with a rough sketch from memory of the structure and appearance of the village and its houses. His next business was to consider some means of identifying the place and the people.

What he had seen was, he felt, not an inevitable event, but the event as it would happen *given those circumstances*. The two men had been alone with every opportunity for quarrel and attack.

The event was set for that hour, and, given the propitious setting, it would happen. But had a third person been present it might have been frustrated; the fit circumstances would have been thrown out of harmony. With his foreknowledge it should be possible for him to disarrange the circumstances, and so put the event out of that particular stream. If he could locate that village and those men, and contrive to make their acquaintance, it should be possible for him to find some excuse for being in their company on the afternoon of September 3rd. And if he were in their company it would be a simple matter to disturb the appointments of the occasion, to change the scene of their meeting, and to see that no hammer or other weapon was in the hand or within reach.

With so clear a picture of the place and people in his mind he felt that he would have little trouble in locating them, since there were yet twelve weeks to go before the foreshadowed event. He set about the business that evening. After casting about for the best method of approaching the task, he remembered a friend who wrote touring notes for a motoring paper. This friend, who spent his days and weeks cruising the highways and byways of England, might be able to provide some clue which would narrow the search; might be able to locate, from Stern's description, the district or the county where such a village might be found. With some such direction, Stern could then start hunting in that district, and he was certain that if he came within sight of the village of his vision he would know it not only by his eyes but by his skin and blood. It remained in his mind as part of an actual experience; as a village he had personally known and walked in; and if he could once get near it he knew that he would feel "warm" and easily find it.

It happened that he had no search for it. Calling his friend on the telephone, he said, "Listen, Jack. I want you to try to remember if you've ever seen on your wanderings a village like this. I'll describe it. I want to find out just where it is, and its name. It's got a green, and on the edge of the green there's a pond, and round the pond there's white railings. The road runs along one side of the green, and the village makes a rough half-circle on the other side. There's a church on one point—Perpendicular—with elms round it."

"That describes four hundred villages."

"Shut up. There's a number of thatched cottages, standing separate here and there, and in between these there's a lot of two-storied houses of late-eighteenth or early-nineteenth-century. White-fronted, and most of 'em have green doors and brass knockers. And they've got those iron verandahs with curved canopies, like you see at old-fashioned seaside places."

"Very lucid. The identical village leaps to the mind at once."

"Don't be silly. Listen. There's just two other points I've got, but they probably won't convey anything. I guess I'll have to see you and show you a sketch I made. Something in the sketch might give you a clue. The points are—that right next to the church there's a white house labelled 'Cranford.' And towards the other end there's a house labelled 'Avoca.' I didn't notice the names of any others, and probably——"

"What was the last one?"

"Avoca."

"Avoca, did you say? Same as Thomas Moore's Sweet Vale of Avoca?"

"Yes."

"And another one called Cranford?"

"Yes."

"Ha! I believe I can work that crossword. Anything else you remember about it?"

"Well, the Cranford house seems to belong to a fellow about fifty. Biggish. Iron-grey. And I believe there's a fellow living at Avoca—fellow in the thirties. Sporty, plus-fours fellow. Reads the *Morning Mercury*——"

"Uh-huh. That'd be the doctor."

"What? You know him?"

"Sounds like the same chap. I've stayed with a plus-fours doctor in his thirties, who lives at a house called Avoca in a village. And he knows a man of the kind you describe who lives in a house next to the church."

"Marvellous. It was a lucky stroke that made me ring you first. Is the village as I describe it?"

"Pretty much. Just an ordinary village. The other details seem to fix it."

"And where is it?

"It's Wayless-Wagtail. In the Thames valley. Why all this interest? Thinking of settling there?"

"No. But I'd be glad if you'd do something for me. Are you likely to be going there within the next week or so?"

"Probably. I see young Winterslow off and on, when it occurs to me."

"Will you take me next time you go and introduce me to him?"

"Well. . . . I could. But why? Don't know that you'd have much in common."

"Perhaps not. But that's one thing I want you to do for me. The other is, not to ask why."

"'M. . . . Sounds all very mysterious."

"You needn't worry. I just want to meet him. It won't do him any damage at all, and it might do him a bit of good. But don't ask why. Just introduce me casually, without any reason. And I'll answer all your questions in a month or so."

"All right. How about Sunday after next? We could drop in for lunch. I'll call for you about eleven."

*　　*　　*　　*

Ten minutes after the car had left the Bath Road a few miles beyond Reading, it turned into a lane, and two minutes later Stern saw in reality the details of the village he had seen in vision on the wall of his book-room. Every detail matched. The green, the pond, the church, the balconied houses and the thatched cottages. By the church he saw "Cranford," with the strip of lawn at the side; and a hundred yards beyond it they came to "Avoca." As the car drew up, the younger man of his vision, Dr. Winterslow, came out to meet them. He was wearing just the sporting tweeds he had worn in the vision; the only difference was that they were fairly new, while in the vision they had clearly had a bit of wear.

During lunch, Stern exerted himself to make an agreeable impression on Winterslow, and felt that he had succeeded. They found a common ground in fishing talk, and it was easy for him to get the invitation to further meetings which he desired. Once an angler finds that a brother-angler doesn't know the local streams, it is seldom that he can resist urging him to come and try them.

No streams afford such catches as an angler's own streams. He was pressed to come for a long week-end, and he foresaw that after that long week-end he would be able to make other visits. He would be able to invite himself for September 3rd, or to drop in casually on the afternoon of that day.

He found Winterslow a pleasant, easy-going fellow, but with something of a tongue. He was looking for some cause of a dispute between the doctor and the elderly man of "Cranford," and he guessed that he had found it in the doctor's tongue. In conversation, he hit off the peculiarities of the village residents in sentences that sounded bland until they were considered, when they revealed little spots of acid. They were remarks such as many people like to repeat to the subject of them, leaving the subject to turn them over and discover the sting. Had Winterslow made a few remarks of that sort about the man at "Cranford," it was certain that a man of his choleric type would resent them more fiercely than open criticism.

Bitterness finds richer ground for growth in villages than in cities. The leisurely days, the restricted social radius, and the lack of new air from the outside to blow away yesterday's echoes, make it easy for a chance remark to breed an enduring feud. Judging by the scene of his vision, and from what he had now learned of Winterslow's caustic turn of mind, something of the sort had happened here. He hoped that some reference to the fiery neighbour might be made during lunch, but though other residents were mentioned, he was left out. Towards the end of the meal Stern tried himself to introduce him.

"Pleasant house, that one next to the church. Regency period, I should say."

"Yes. They knew how to design houses and rooms in those days. And how to fit their design to the surroundings."

"Anybody interesting own it?"

"No-o. Just a type. Type you find in every village. Sun-dried sahib from India's coral strand. The Bombay Duck. A strip of dried fish. With as much individuality as all the other strips of dried fish. And speaking of fish, what about that week-end? Perhaps we could fix it now."

⋆   ⋆   ⋆   ⋆

Having made the week-end visit, Stern found himself, as he had expected with so easy-going a fellow as Winterslow, invited to "drop in any time." To keep the acquaintance warm until September, he dropped in twice between June and the middle of August, and at about that time he invited himself for the second of September, with the suggestion of staying the night.

He arrived on the evening of the second, with the details of his vision still fresh in his mind. He had no clear plan of how he would handle the situation next day, if it arose—and he believed it would; he decided that he must await the event and take his cue from any chance that offered. The one point on which he was clear was that he must not let Winterslow out of his sight at any time of next afternoon.

The situation did arise. Winterslow himself took the first step towards the death foretold for him in the vision; the death that Stern was there to avert. Soon after lunch he asked Stern: "Care for a stroll? Don't think you've seen our church. Not much interested in ecclesiastical stuff myself, but they say there's some fine Norman work in it, and one specially good window. And a couple of fine marbles which I do think are worth seeing." For a moment Stern hesitated whether to suggest a stroll in some other direction, or to fall in with the idea and let Winterslow enter the situation and be saved from its climax by his own presence. If he took Winterslow in another direction, it might mean merely postponing the meeting of the two men, and the incident of the vision might work itself out on a later occasion. If it were met at its appointed time it might, *barring accidents*, be thwarted.

His hesitation was settled by Winterslow, who picked up from a chair that day's *Morning Mercury*. "Just take this along. Article in here that might interest the old Bombay Duck. We shall be passing his place."

As they went along the green, Stern noted that the scene was precisely the scene of his vision. The time was exact; the fall of the sunlight, the movement of cloud, the light breeze on the tree-tops—all were as he had seen them. Even the ducks on the pond were distributed as he remembered them, and when they were half-way towards the church the flight of a rook across the skyline made current fact of another point of the vision. When they neared the church—and "Cranford"—Stern found his pulse increasing. The event was now very close, but the lawn of "Cranford" was empty; and he wondered whether perhaps his presence had already thrown the thing out of adjustment. For a moment he felt as a child feels when it puts the penny in the slot of the mechanical-farmyard machine, and wonders whether it really will come to life, as promised.

Then the door of "Cranford" snapped open, and out came its florid, iron-grey owner, carrying nails and hammer. Stern caught his breath, and waited for the next move. Winterslow made it. As the man began work on the fence they reached his gate, and Winterslow pushed it open and entered. Stern followed close behind him. His eye and brain were set on every turn of the succeeding seconds.

The sound of their steps brought a glance from the man, but he went on hammering, until Winterslow was near him. "Seen to-day's *Mercury*, Colonel?" He stepped back from the fence then, still swinging the hammer, and faced them.

"No, sir. I read papers written by adults for adults."

"Aha." Winterslow was unabashed by his reception. "You like the old dignities, eh? The old English journalism. But we live in American times now. Everything young and swift. Still, you'll admit, I think, that Lord Simla's an adult where India's concerned. Interesting article by him on the situation in the *Mercury*. Thought you might like to see it."

"Thank you, sir; no. I don't care to have papers of that sort about my place." Stern, watching them closely, saw in the Colonel's eyes an expression which seemed to finish the sentence with "nor people of your sort about my place."

"All right, then. I just thought you might be interested."

"I'm not. And listen, Doctor Winterslow"—swinging the hammer—"I'd like a word with you."

"Sure."

The Colonel moved to the open door and into the hall. Winterslow followed. Stern followed, too. The Colonel stared—or rather, glared—at him. The glare said, "Impertinent intruder

—get out." Stern accepted the glare and remained close by Winterslow. The Colonel then seemed to think that his "word" to Winterslow might be a little more, rather than a little less, effective if delivered in the presence of a third party. He turned from the third party with, "Look here, Winterslow, I want to know——" when the third party earned for himself a fiercer glare by interrupting him.

Stern took a pace towards him, and committed a graver impertinence. "What an unusual kind of hammer, sir."

"Unusual, sir? I don't see anything unusual about it."

"Is it Indian?"

"No, sir, it's not Indian. Nor Chinese. Nor Afghan. It's a hammer."

"But really, sir—excuse me—if I may——" Ignoring the boiling of the Colonel's face, he reached forward and took the hammer from the Colonel's hand. The Colonel, unaware that in that moment he was being saved from the brand of murderer, let it go, mainly because he was taken by surprise at the fellow's sheer audacity. Ten seconds later when he was prepared with protest, the fellow was babbling about hammers.

"No, it's not so unusual as I thought. It was just something in the form of the claw that I thought was different. I'm rather interested in tools. It's odd that the everyday tools of man have scarcely changed from their beginnings. Most of the hammers of to-day are of the same style as the earliest hammers you find in museums. Farm-carts, too. Practically the same as you see in the earliest English decorations. The hammer must be the primary tool of man, I fancy, though it offers a parallel to the problem of the chicken and the egg—which came first: the hammer or the nail? The hammer——" Stern had no idea what he was saying or what words he was finding; he was talking merely to cover his action in taking the hammer and to hold the situation. He finished lamely. "Forgive my blithering on like this. You wanted to give the doctor a message, I think."

"I did. And the message is—that I don't wish to put him to the trouble of making further calls on me. He's a nuisance to the village. A nuisance. As he says, I prefer the old dignities. I've no use for the young impudences."

Winterslow looked first surprised; then angry. "Really, Colonel. . . . Something's wrong with you this afternoon. I thought you were rather frigid when I came in."

"Frigid? I'm always frigid, sir, with Bounders."

"Are you talking to me?" Winterslow's shoulders came forward. "I know you're a hot-tempered old man, but——" He took a step towards the Colonel. The Colonel lifted his arm. Stern, holding the hammer, stepped between them. "Please . . . please. I don't know what the trouble is, but——"

"The trouble is, sir, that your friend, if he is your friend, is an impudent fellow. Gibing at his betters. A thorough nuisance." The Colonel's heat seemed to cool in shooting his sentences at a third party. "I don't know who you are, and I don't recall inviting you in. But since you're here you can do something for me. You can take your friend away."

Winterslow looked as though he had something blandly mordant to say, and was about to say it when Stern caught his eye, and made a furtive signal conveying weighty and mysterious business in the garden. Winterslow looked at him, and at the Colonel, and said, "Oh, all right; anything for a quiet life," and strolled out with Stern. The Colonel slammed the door on them.

"Nice chap," Winterslow said. "Nice chap, isn't he, the Bombay Duck? What's going on in the garden?"

"Nothing, that I know of."

"What were you making that wild signal for, then? I thought you meant there was something doing out here."

"No; I only wanted to get you out of that brawl."

"I see. Probably would have developed into that. If he'd said much more I really believe I'd have gone for him. Don't know what's got him this afternoon to set him on me. Looked quite murderous. But you never know, with these old boys. Synthetic products of chutney and curry and hell-fire foods. . . . I say, you've got the old boy's hammer. You'll lead him right into murder if he sees you."

Stern looked down and found he was still carrying the hammer. He went back a few paces and dropped it by the broken fence. When he rejoined Winterslow at the gate, the young man, in his easy-going habit, seemed to have forgotten the ugly scene.

He began talking about the marbles in the church.

*   *   *   *

Late in the following year, when Stern was sunk in his real work, and had wholly forgotten the human duty he had performed for a comparative stranger, he was called to the telephone. His touring friend was speaking.

"Oh, Stern—remember that place you wanted to know all about some time ago. Where you met the doctor chap and went fishing two or three times. Wayless-Wagtail. . . . Well, I was there this afternoon, and as you seemed fond of the place, and knew the people, I thought you might like to know."

"Know what?"

"Oh, there was a bit of a mess-up there this afternoon. And our friend, the doctor chap, was in it. Winterslow."

"Winter—— Oh, yes—I remember. A mess-up, you say? How? What sort?"

"Oh, sudden death. Outside the church. They were having what we call Words. And he just went over and out."

"What—Winterslow? Who struck him? I suppose it was——"

"No. The old Colonel Johnny."

"The *Colonel*, did you say? Not Winterslow?"

"Of course not. He's healthy enough. No—the Colonel. Tried to swipe at Winterslow, and went down and out. Heart failure. Winterslow said he tried to do it the same day a year ago. When you were there."

THE HOLLOW MAN

He came up one of the narrow streets which lead from the docks, and turned into a road whose farther end was gay with the lights of London. At the end of this road he went deep into the lights of London, and sometimes into its shadows. Farther and farther he went from the river, and did not pause until he had reached a poor quarter near the centre.

He made a tall, spare figure, clothed in a black mackintosh. Below this could be seen brown dungaree trousers. A peaked cap hid most of his face; the little that was exposed was white and sharp. In the autumn mist that filled the lighted streets as well as the dark he seemed a wraith, and some of those who passed him looked again, not sure whether they had indeed seen a living man. One or two of them moved their shoulders, as though shrinking from something.

His legs were long, but he walked with the short, deliberate steps of a blind man, though he was not blind. His eyes were open, and he stared straight ahead; but he seemed to see nothing and hear nothing. Neither the mournful hooting of sirens across the black water of the river, nor the genial windows of the shops in the big streets near the centre drew his head to right or left. He walked as though he had no destination in mind, yet constantly, at this corner or that, he turned. It seemed that an unseen hand was guiding him to a given point of whose location he was himself ignorant.

He was searching for a friend of fifteen years ago, and the unseen hand, or some dog-instinct, had led him from Africa to London, and was now leading him, along the last mile of his search, to a certain little eating-house. He did not know that he was going to the eating-house of his friend Nameless, but he did know, from the time he left Africa, that he was journeying towards Nameless, and he now knew that he was very near to Nameless.

Nameless didn't know that his old friend was anywhere near *him*, though, had he observed conditions that evening, he might have wondered why he was sitting up an hour later than usual. He was seated in one of the pews of his prosperous Workmen's Dining-Rooms—a little gold-mine his wife's relations called it— and he was smoking and looking at nothing. He had added up the till and written the copies of the bill of fare for next day, and there was nothing to keep him out of bed after his fifteen hours' attention to business. Had he been asked why he was sitting up later than usual, he would first have answered that he didn't know that he was, and would then have explained, in default of any other explanation, that it was for the purpose of having a last pipe. He was quite unaware that he was sitting up and keeping the door unlatched because a long-parted friend from Africa was seeking him and slowly approaching him, and needed his services. He was quite unaware that he had left the door unlatched at that late hour—half-past eleven—to admit pain and woe.

But even as many bells sent dolefully across the night from their steeples their disagreement as to the point of half-past eleven, pain and woe were but two streets away from him. The mackintosh and dungarees and the sharp white face were coming nearer every moment.

There was silence in the house and in the streets; a heavy silence, broken, or sometimes stressed, by the occasional night-noises—motor horns, back-firing of lorries, shunting at a distant terminus. That silence seemed to envelop the house, but he did not notice it. He did not notice the bells, and he did not even notice the lagging step that approached his shop, and passed— and returned—and passed again—and halted. He was aware of nothing save that he was smoking a last pipe, and he was sitting in somnolence, deaf and blind to anything not in his immediate neighbourhood.

But when a hand was laid on the latch, and the latch was lifted, he did hear that, and he looked up. And he saw the door open, and got up and went to it. And there, just within the door, he came face to face with the thin figure of pain and woe.

*   *   *   *

To kill a fellow-creature is a frightful thing. At the time the act is committed the murderer may have sound and convincing reasons (to him) for his act. But time and reflection may bring regret; even remorse; and this may live with him for many years. Examined in wakeful hours of the night or early morning, the reasons for the act may shed their cold logic, and may cease to be reasons and become mere excuses. And these naked excuses may strip the murderer and show him to himself as he is. They may begin to hunt his soul, and to run into every little corner of his mind and every little nerve, in search of it.

And if to kill a fellow-creature and to suffer recurrent regret for an act of heated blood is a frightful thing, it is still more frightful to kill a fellow-creature and bury his body deep in an African jungle, and then, fifteen years later, at about midnight, to see the latch of your door lifted by the hand you had stilled and to see the man, looking much as he did fifteen years ago, walk into your home and claim your hospitality.

*　　*　　*　　*

When the man in mackintosh and dungarees walked into the dining-rooms Nameless stood still; stared; staggered against a table; supported himself by a hand, and said, "Oh."

The other man said, "Nameless."

Then they looked at each other; Nameless with head thrust forward, mouth dropped, eyes wide; the visitor with a dull, glazed expression. If Nameless had not been the man he was— thick, bovine and costive—he would have flung up his arms and screamed. At that moment he felt the need of some such outlet, but did not know how to find it. The only dramatic expression he gave to the situation was to whisper instead of speak.

Twenty emotions came to life in his head and spine, and wrestled there. But they showed themselves only in his staring eyes and his whisper. His first thought, or rather, spasm, was Ghosts-Indigestion-Nervous-Breakdown. His second, when he saw that the figure was substantial and real, was Impersonation. But a slight movement on the part of the visitor dismissed that.

It was a little habitual movement which belonged only to that man; an unconscious twitching of the third finger of the left hand. He knew then that it was Gopak. Gopak, a little changed, but still, miraculously, thirty-two. Gopak, alive, breathing and real. No ghost. No phantom of the stomach. He was as certain of that as he was that fifteen years ago he had killed Gopak stone-dead and buried him.

The blackness of the moment was lightened by Gopak. In thin, flat tones he asked, "May I sit down? I'm tired." He sat down, and said: "So tired."

Nameless still held the table. He whispered: "Gopak. . . . Gopak. . . . But I—I *killed* you. I killed you in the jungle. You were dead. I know you were."

Gopak passed his hand across his face. He seemed about to cry. "I know you did. I know. That's all I can remember—about this earth. You killed me." The voice became thinner and flatter. "And then they came and—disturbed me. They woke me up. And brought me back." He sat with shoulders sagged, arms drooping, hands hanging between knees. After the first recognition he did not look at Nameless; he looked at the floor.

"Came and disturbed you?" Nameless leaned forward and whispered the words. "Woke you up? Who?"

"The Leopard Men."

"The what?"

"The Leopard Men." The watery voice said it as casually as if it were saying "the night watchman."

"The Leopard Men?" Nameless stared, and his fat face crinkled in an effort to take in the situation of a midnight visitation from a dead man, and the dead man talking nonsense. He felt his blood moving out of its course. He looked at his own hand to see if it was his own hand. He looked at the table to see if it was his table. The hand and the table were facts, and if the dead man was a fact—and he was—his story might be a fact. It seemed anyway as sensible as the dead man's presence. He gave a heavy sigh from the stomach. "A-ah. . . . The Leopard Men. . . . Yes, I heard about them out there. Tales."

Gopak slowly wagged his head. "Not tales. They're real. If they weren't real—I wouldn't be here. Would I?"

Nameless had to admit this. He had heard many tales "out

there" about the Leopard Men, and had dismissed them as jungle yarns. But now, it seemed, jungle yarns had become commonplace fact in a little London shop. The watery voice went on. "They do it. I saw them. I came back in the middle of a circle of them. They killed a nigger to put his life into me. They wanted a white man—for their farm. So they brought me back. You may not believe it. You wouldn't *want* to believe it. You wouldn't want to—see or know anything like them. And I wouldn't want any man to. But it's true. That's how I'm here."

"But I left you absolutely dead. I made every test. It was three days before I buried you. And I buried you deep."

"I know. But that wouldn't make any difference to them. It was a long time after when they came and brought me back. And I'm still dead, you know. It's only my body they brought back." The voice trailed into a thread. "And I'm so tired."

Sitting in his prosperous eating-house Nameless was in the presence of an achieved miracle, but the everyday, solid appointments of the eating-house wouldn't let him fully comprehend it. Foolishly, as he realized when he had spoken, he asked Gopak to explain what had happened. Asked a man who couldn't really be alive to explain how he came to be alive. It was like asking Nothing to explain Everything.

Constantly, as he talked, he felt his grasp on his own mind slipping. The surprise of a sudden visitor at a late hour; the shock of the arrival of a long-dead man; and the realization that this long-dead man was not a wraith, were too much for him.

During the next half-hour he found himself talking to Gopak as to the Gopak he had known seventeen years ago when they were partners. Then he would be halted by the freezing knowledge that he was talking to a dead man, and that a dead man was faintly answering him. He felt that the thing couldn't really have happened, but in the interchange of talk he kept forgetting the improbable side of it, and accepting it. With each recollection of the truth, his mind would clear and settle in one thought—"I've got to get rid of him. How am I going to get rid of him?"

"But how did you get here?"

"I escaped." The words came slowly and thinly, and out of the body rather than the mouth.

"How?"

"I don't—know. I don't remember anything—except our quarrel. And being at rest."

"But why come all the way here? Why didn't you stay on the coast?"

"I don't—know. But you're the only man I know. The only man I can remember."

"But how did you find me?"

"I don't know. But I had to—find you. You're the only man—who can help me."

"But how can I help you?"

The head turned weakly from side to side. "I don't—know. But nobody else—can."

Nameless stared through the window, looking on to the lamplit street and seeing nothing of it. The everyday being which had been his half an hour ago had been annihilated; the everyday beliefs and disbeliefs shattered and mixed together. But some shred of his old sense and his old standards remained. He must handle this situation. "Well—what you want to do? What you going to do? I don't see how I can help you. And you can't stay here, obviously." A demon of perversity sent a facetious notion into his head—introducing Gopak to his wife—"This is my dead friend."

But on his last spoken remark Gopak made the effort of raising his head and staring with the glazed eyes at Nameless. "But I *must* stay here. There's nowhere else I can stay. I must stay here. That's why I came. You got to help me."

"But you can't stay here. I got no room. All occupied. Nowhere for you to sleep."

The wan voice said: "That doesn't matter. I *don't* sleep."

"Eh?"

"I *don't* sleep. I haven't slept since they brought me back. I can sit here—till you can think of some way of helping me."

"But how *can* I?" He again forgot the background of the situation, and began to get angry at the vision of a dead man sitting about the place waiting for him to think of something. "How *can* I if you don't tell me how?"

"I don't—know. But you got to. You killed me. And I was dead

—and comfortable. As it all came from you—killing me—you're responsible for me being—like this. So you got to—help me. That's why I—came to you."

"But what do you want me to do?"

"I don't—know. I can't—think. But nobody but you can help me. I had to come to you. Something brought me—straight to you. That means that you're the one—that can help me. Now I'm with you, something will—happen to help me. I feel it will. In time you'll—think of something."

Nameless found his legs suddenly weak. He sat down and stared with a sick scowl at the hideous and the incomprehensible. Here was a dead man in his house—a man he had murdered in a moment of black temper—and he knew in his heart that he couldn't turn the man out. For one thing, he would have been afraid to touch him; he couldn't see himself touching him. For another, faced with the miracle of the presence of a fifteen-years-dead man, he doubted whether physical force or any material agency would be effectual in moving the man.

His soul shivered, as all men's souls shiver at the demonstration of forces outside their mental or spiritual horizon. He had murdered this man, and often, in fifteen years, he had repented the act. If the man's appalling story were true, then he had some sort of right to turn to Nameless. Nameless recognised that, and knew that whatever happened he couldn't turn him out. His hot-tempered sin had literally come home to him.

The wan voice broke into his nightmare. "You go to rest, Nameless. I'll sit here. You go to rest." He put his face down to his hands and uttered a little moan. "Oh, why can't I rest?"

*   *   *   *

Nameless came down early next morning with a half-hope that Gopak would not be there. But he was there, seated where Nameless had left him last night. Nameless made some tea, and showed him where he might wash. He washed listlessly, and crawled back to his seat, and listlessly drank the tea which Nameless brought to him.

To his wife and the kitchen helpers Nameless mentioned him as an old friend who had had a bit of a shock. "Shipwrecked and knocked on the head. But quite harmless, and he won't be staying long. He's waiting for admission to a home. A good pal to me in the past, and it's the least I can do to let him stay here a few days. Suffers from sleeplessness and prefers to sit up at night. Quite harmless."

But Gopak stayed more than a few days. He outstayed everybody. Even when the customers had gone Gopak was still there.

On the first morning of his visit when the regular customers came in at mid-day, they looked at the odd, white figure sitting vacantly in the first pew, then stared, then moved away. All avoided the pew in which he sat. Nameless explained him to them, but his explanation did not seem to relieve the slight tension which settled on the dining-room. The atmosphere was not so brisk and chatty as usual. Even those who had their backs to the stranger seemed to be affected by his presence.

At the end of the first day Nameless, noticing this, told him that he had arranged a nice corner of the front-room upstairs, where he could sit by the window, and took his arm to take him upstairs. But Gopak feebly shook the hand away, and sat where he was. "No. I don't want to go. I'll stay here. I'll stay here. I don't want to move."

And he wouldn't move. After a few more pleadings Nameless realized with dismay that his refusal was definite; that it would be futile to press him or force him; that he was going to sit in that dining-room for ever. He was as weak as a child and as firm as a rock. He continued to sit in that first pew, and the customers continued to avoid it, and to give queer glances at it. It seemed that they half-recognized that he was something more than a fellow who had had a shock.

During the second week of his stay three of the regular customers were missing, and more than one of those that remained made acidly facetious suggestions to Nameless that he park his lively friend somewhere else. He made things too exciting for them; all that whoopee took them off their work, and interfered with digestion. Nameless told them he would be staying only a day or so longer, but they found that this was untrue, and at the end of the second week eight of the regulars had found another place.

Each day, when the dinner-hour came, Nameless tried to get him to take a little walk, but always he refused. He would go out only at night, and then never more than two hundred yards from the shop. For the rest, he sat in his pew, sometimes dozing in the afternoon, at other times staring at the floor. He took his food abstractedly, and never knew whether he had had food or not. He spoke only when questioned, and the burden of his talk was "I'm so tired."

One thing only seemed to arouse any light of interest in him; one thing only drew his eyes from the floor. That was the seventeen-year-old daughter of his host, who was known as Bubbles, and who helped with the waiting. And Bubbles seemed to be the only member of the shop and its customers who did not shrink from him.

She knew nothing of the truth about him, but she seemed to understand him, and the only response he ever gave to anything was to her childish sympathy. She sat and chatted foolish chatter to him—"bringing him out of himself," she called it—and sometimes he would be brought out to the extent of a watery smile. He came to recognize her step, and would look up before she entered the room. Once or twice in the evening, when the shop was empty, and Nameless was sitting miserably with him, he would ask, without lifting his eyes, "Where's Bubbles?" and would be told that Bubbles had gone to the pictures or was out at a dance, and would relapse into deeper vacancy.

Nameless didn't like this. He was already visited by a curse which, in four weeks, had destroyed most of his business. Regular customers had dropped off two by two, and no new customers came to take their place. Strangers who dropped in once for a meal did not come again; they could not keep their eyes or their minds off the forbidding, white-faced figure sitting motionless in the first pew. At mid-day, when the place had been crowded and latecomers had to wait for a seat, it was now two-thirds empty; only a few of the most thick-skinned remained faithful.

And on top of this there was the interest of the dead man in his daughter, an interest which seemed to be having an unpleasant effect. Nameless hadn't noticed it, but his wife had. "Bubbles don't seem as bright and lively as she was. You noticed it lately?

She's getting quiet—and a bit slack. Sits about a lot. Paler than she used to be."

"Her age, perhaps."

"No. She's not one of these thin dark sort. No—it's something else. Just the last week or two I've noticed it. Off her food. Sits about doing nothing. No interest. May be nothing—just out of sorts, perhaps. . . . How much longer's that horrible friend of yours going to stay?"

* * * *

The horrible friend stayed some weeks longer—ten weeks in all—while Nameless watched his business drop to nothing and his daughter get pale and peevish. He knew the cause of it. There was no home in all England like his: no home that had a dead man sitting in it for ten weeks. A dead man brought, after a long time, from the grave, to sit and disturb his customers and take the vitality from his daughter. He couldn't tell this to anybody. Nobody would believe such nonsense. But he *knew* that he was entertaining a dead man, and, knowing that a long-dead man was walking the earth, he could believe in any result of that fact. He could believe almost anything that he would have derided ten weeks ago. His customers had abandoned his shop, not because of the presence of a silent, white-faced man, but because of the presence of a dead-living man. Their minds might not know it, but their blood knew it. And, as his business had been destroyed, so, he believed, would his daughter be destroyed. Her blood was not warning her; her blood told her only that this was a long-ago friend of her father's, and she was drawn to him.

It was at this point that Nameless, having no work to do, began to drink. And it was well that he did so. For out of the drink came an idea, and with that idea he freed himself from the curse upon him and his house.

The shop now served scarcely half a dozen customers at mid-day. It had become ill-kempt and dusty, and the service and the food were bad. Nameless took no trouble to be civil to his few customers. Often, when he was notably under drink, he went to the trouble of being very rude to them. They talked about this. They talked about the decline of his business and the dustiness of the shop and the bad food. They talked about his drinking, and, of course, exaggerated it.

And they talked about the queer fellow who sat there day after day and gave everybody the creeps. A few outsiders, hearing the gossip, came to the dining-rooms to see the queer fellow and the always-tight proprietor; but they did not come again, and there were not enough of the curious to keep the place busy. It went down until it served scarcely two customers a day. And Nameless went down with it into drink.

Then, one evening, out of the drink he fished an inspiration.

He took it downstairs to Gopak, who was sitting in his usual seat, hands hanging, eyes on the floor. "Gopak—listen. You came here because I was the only man who could help you in your trouble. You listening?"

A faint "Yes" was his answer.

"Well, now. You told me I'd got to think of something. I've thought of something. . . . Listen. You say I'm responsible for your condition and got to get you out of it, because I killed you. I did. We had a row. You made me wild. You dared me. And what with that sun and the jungle and the insects, I wasn't meself. I killed you. The moment it was done I could 'a cut me right hand off. Because you and me were pals. I could 'a cut me right hand off."

"I know. I felt that directly it was over. I knew you were suffering."

"Ah! . . . I have suffered. And I'm suffering now. Well, this is what I've thought. All your present trouble comes from me killing you in that jungle and burying you. An idea came to me. Do you think it would help you—I—if I—if I—killed you again?"

For some seconds Gopak continued to stare at the floor. Then his shoulders moved. Then, while Nameless watched every little response to his idea, the watery voice began. "Yes. Yes. That's it. That's what I was waiting for. That's why I came here. I can see now. That's why I had to get here. Nobody else could kill me. Only you. I've got to be killed again. Yes, I see. But nobody else—would be able—to kill me. Only the man who first killed me. . . . Yes, you've found—what we're both—waiting for. Anybody else could shoot me—stab me—hang me—but they couldn't kill me.

Only you. That's why I managed to get here and find you." The watery voice rose to a thin strength. "That's it. And you must do it. Do it now. You don't want to, I know. But you must. You *must.*"

His head drooped and he stared at the floor. Nameless, too, stared at the floor. He was seeing things. He had murdered a man and had escaped all punishment save that of his own mind, which had been terrible enough. But now he was going to murder him again—not in a jungle but in a city; and he saw the slow points of the result.

He saw the arrest. He saw the first hearing. He saw the trial. He saw the cell. He saw the rope. He shuddered.

Then he saw the alternative—the breakdown of his life—a ruined business, poverty, the poor-house, a daughter robbed of her health and perhaps dying, and always the curse of the dead-living man, who might follow him to the poor-house. Better to end it all, he thought. Rid himself of the curse which Gopak had brought upon him and his family, and then rid his family of himself with a revolver. Better to follow up his idea.

He got stiffly to his feet. The hour was late evening—half-past ten—and the streets were quiet. He had pulled down the shop-blinds and locked the door. The room was lit by one light at the farther end. He moved about uncertainly and looked at Gopak. "Er—how would you—how shall I——"

Gopak said, "You did it with a knife. Just under the heart. You must do it that way again."

Nameless stood and looked at him for some seconds. Then, with an air of resolve, he shook himself. He walked quickly to the kitchen.

Three minutes later his wife and daughter heard a crash, as though a table had been overturned. They called but got no answer. When they came down they found him sitting in one of the pews, wiping sweat from his forehead. He was white and shaking, and appeared to be recovering from a faint.

"Whatever's the matter? You all right?"

He waved them away. "Yes, I'm all right. Touch of giddiness. Smoking too much, I think."

"Mmmm. Or drinking.... Where's your friend? Out for a walk?"

"No. He's gone off. Said he wouldn't impose any longer, and 'd go and find an infirmary." He spoke weakly and found trouble in picking words. "Didn't you hear that bang—when he shut the door?"

"I thought that was you fell down."

"No. It was him when he went. I couldn't stop him."

"Mmmm. Just as well, I think." She looked about her. "Things seem to 'a gone all wrong since he's been here."

There was a general air of dustiness about the place. The table-cloths were dirty, not from use but from disuse. The windows were dim. A long knife, very dusty, was lying on the table under the window. In a corner by the door leading to the kitchen, unseen by her, lay a dusty mackintosh and dungaree, which appeared to have been tossed there. But it was over by the main door, near the first pew, that the dust was thickest—a long trail of it—greyish-white dust.

"Reely this place gets more and more slapdash. Just *look* at that dust by the door. Looks as though somebody's been spilling ashes all over the place."

Nameless looked at it, and his hands shook a little. But he answered, more firmly than before: "Yes, I know. I'll have a proper clean-up to-morrow."

For the first time in ten weeks he smiled at them; a thin, haggard smile, but a smile.

CPSIA information can be obtained at www.ICGtesting.com
Printed in the USA
BVOW02s0753130116

432701BV00004B/136/P